DEPARTURES

Praise for Tony Parsons:

'Tony Parsons gets inside the heads and hearts of modern men'
The Times

'Parsons manages to astutely cut right to the heart of family life'
Woman and Home

'Unashamedly touching . . . funny and well-written'
Telegraph magazine

'Memorable and poignant – nobody squeezes more genuine emotion from a scene than Tony Parsons'
Spectator

'One of the many great things about a Tony Parsons novel is that they always make you feel not just alive, but even more aware of how precious life is . . .'
Mirror

By the same author

Man and Boy
One For My Baby
Man and Wife
The Family Way
Stories We Could Tell
My Favourite Wife
Starting Over
Men from the Boys

Tony Parsons on Life, Death and Breakfast

Coming Soon

Catching the Sun
Beyond the Bounty (Quick Read)

TONY PARSONS

Departures

Seven stories from Heathrow

HARPER

Harper
An imprint of HarperCollins*Publishers*
77–85 Fulham Palace Road,
Hammersmith, London W6 8JB

www.harpercollins.co.uk

First published in Great Britain by
HarperCollins*Publishers* 2011
1

A catalogue record for this book is
available from the British Library

ISBN: 978 0 00 745865 3

Set in Sabon by Palimpsest Book Production Limited,
Falkirk, Stirlingshire

Printed and bound in Great Britain by
Clays Ltd, St Ives plc

FSC™ is a non-profit international organisation established to promote
the responsible management of the world's forests. Products carrying the
FSC label are independently certified to assure consumers that they come
from forests that are managed to meet the social, economic and
ecological needs of present and future generations,
and other controlled sources.

Find out more about HarperCollins and the environment at
www.harpercollins.co.uk/green

For David Morrison, Barry Hoy and Kevin Steele
Somewhere East of Suez

'The midnight plane with its flying lights
Looks like an unloosed star
Wandering west through the blue-black night
To where the mountains are.'
Frances Frost, 'Night Plane'

One

The Green Plane

She was not a weak woman.

As she stood at the window, watching the pale blue sky and looking back on her twenty-nine years of life, Zoe could see no evidence that she was weak, timid, or what her three elder brothers would have sneeringly called a 'wuss'.

When a girl grows up heavily outnumbered by brothers, Zoe thought, she learns to take the knocks, and never to let them see you cry, and always to be tougher than they expect.

Zoe had done all of that, and then when her brothers were all grown and gone and getting on with their lives, and she could have relaxed a little bit on the whole acting tough thing, she had spent a gap year wandering Asia alone (her best friend was meant to come but she met a boy – it was that old story). Zoe had ridden a prehistoric rented motorbike from Hanoi to Ho Chi Minh City, shivered with dysentery in Mumbai, and when the money ran out – Japan had been more expensive than she was antici-pating – she had slept rough in a park in Kyoto while

1

waiting for her parents to send her the fare to come home.

I am not weak, she thought, so vehemently that she almost said it out loud. I'm not, I'm not, I'm not.

But, as she stared at the sky, a small black line appeared against the perfect blue, as thin as a razor cut, and she felt her breath shorten and the sweat break out and the panic fly.

It moved so slowly. Though the plane must have been going at, what – 500 mph or so? – it seemed to move in slow motion as it crossed the London skyline, and then languidly turned, as if ready to meet its fate.

Zoe was not a woman who scared easily.

But Zoe was afraid of flying.

'Angel?'

She turned from the window to look at her husband. He was sitting at the kitchen table, their three-year-old girl on his knees, attempting to keep her sticky little fingers away from the laptop in front of him.

'It says here,' he said, 'that twenty-five per cent of people have some fear of flying and around ten per cent have a real psychological phobia.'

'But I'm not afraid of flying,' Zoe insisted.

In the silence her husband, Nick, and their daughter, Sky, smiled at her sympathetically, as if forgiving her this blatant lie.

Nick returned to the computer. Sky banged her small hands on the keyboard as if it was a toy piano. Nick gathered both of the child's hands in one of his own, and pointed at the screen with an enthusiastic grin that somehow made Zoe's spirits sink.

'They do courses for people who, er, don't like to fly,' he said. 'British Airways had a course called Fear of Flying – please don't do that, darling' (this to his daughter) '– and now they call it, um, Flying With Confidence.'

Zoe laughed bitterly. 'That's a smart move. Flying With Confidence sounds a lot more positive than Fear of bloody Flying.'

Nick looked hurt. 'But that's a good thing, isn't it? To be positive about the . . . aversion.'

'They make it sound irrational,' she said. '*You* make it sound irrational. All those hundreds of people locked inside a metal tube above the clouds. Maybe it's you that's crazy for not being . . . a little bit . . . worried? You ever think about that, Nick? Maybe it's you and the rest of the flying glee club. Maybe I'm the sane one.'

She turned back to the window. There were a few of them up there now – their west London home was directly under a flight path – moving like deep black wounds in the sky. So slowly, so slowly. As if they could fall at any moment. She wiped her hands on her jeans, and it all came back.

The noises that sounded like the end of everything. The engines starting – that screaming sound that froze the blood. The suicidal dash to the end of the runway. The mad sensation of leaving solid ground. Rising, rising, like the nausea in the pit of your stomach. And then – perhaps worst of all – the sound of the undercarriage being lifted, as final as the lid on your coffin slamming shut and the nails being banged in. That was the moment you knew there was no going back.

You were trapped.

Then Nick was by her side, Sky in his arms. The girl slipped from the arms of her father to her mother, the way monkeys and small children do.

'I just want to help,' Nick said.

She put her free arm around him.

'I know you do,' she said. 'But the thing is, Nick – I really don't have a fear of flying.'

He looked uncertain. 'You don't?'

'It's just that I have a problem with take-off and landing,' she said. Then paused. 'And the bit in the middle.'

'One of these courses can help,' he said. 'I believe it. There are lots of people who feel like you, Zoe. You're right – it's not a mad way to feel. On these courses, pilots talk to you. They explain the sounds. I know you don't like the sounds . . .'

She suddenly lit up.

'Or we could do something else,' she said excitedly.

'Yes?'

'Stay home,' she said, jiggling the child in her arms, making her laugh, and smiling herself now. 'We could just stay home, Nick. Not go.'

Nick stared at his wife for a long moment.

And then he shook his head.

'But we have to go,' he said.

The green plane burned.

The engine burned. The cockpit burned. The green

plane burned in the galley and it burned in the under-carriage and it burned in the brakes.

The green plane burned more wildly as the firefighters jumped from the two fire engines – rigs, they called them, and they did not look like anyone's idea of a fire engine. These fire engines, these rigs, looked more solid, more tank-like, and more ready for a war than a normal fire engine. They were built to go in a straight line. From one of two fire stations at either end of Heathrow to an aircraft in trouble. Like the green plane.

An oil spill spread quickly under the two sawn-off wings of the green plane, and that burned too, a sheet of fire that swiftly rose to a spectacular wall of flame, trailing black smoke as the four firefighters advanced towards it, crouching before the terrible heat, tasting it in the back of their throats, the hoses in their hands looking like small, ineffectual weapons, plastic swords against a dragon, until the moment they began covering the fire with foam, starving it of the air that it craved, choking it, killing it.

In one of the two rigs that faced the nose of the green plane, unloading their blankets of foam on top of the fire, Fire Officer Mike Truman watched the proceedings with quiet satisfaction.

Mike had watched Heathrow's green plane burn hundreds of times. It was a strange-looking hybrid, made up of many aircraft. The tail of a DC-10. The fuselage of a Jumbo. Bits and pieces all combined into one so that the Heathrow Airport fire service could be prepared for any fire on any aircraft at any time.

Burning the green plane was a drill. Aircraft use Jet A-1 aviation fuel, a hydrocarbon fuel, whereas the green plane's fires were gas. And aircraft are constructed of sheet aluminium, or more recently lightweight plastics reinforced with man-made mineral fibres known as composites, and the green plane was built of steel. It was just a drill. But there were twenty-six different scenarios on the green plane – twenty-six different ways for it to burn. So it was a drill that prepared the fire-fighters of Heathrow for anything.

When the green plane had arrived at the airport at the end of the last century, the same year as Mike, it had been as immaculate as a brand-spanking new car fresh off the assembly line. The green had shone in those days, like a pair of Robin Hood's freshly washed tights.

Now, after the countless fires that Mike and his firefighters had started, the green plane was definitely showing its age. There were scars. There was wear and tear. It looked a bit rough. Just like me, Mike thought, grinning to himself.

Then he looked at the sky and frowned.

A big, blue cloudless sky hung above Heathrow. It was a beautiful day, he reflected with distaste. And that, thought Mike Truman, was the only thing that stopped this being a perfect drill.

He liked to see the green plane burn when the weather was filthy. He liked it when the light was bad, and the rigs sprayed rain or slush from their wheels as they raced to an incident.

An aircraft, he always reminded his men, contains

enough fuel to fill five oil tankers. Imagine – just imagine, he would tell them – what that lot looks like when it is on fire. An aircraft is an unexploded bomb with five hundred people sitting inside it. And our job is to keep them all safe from harm.

So you didn't want good weather when you burned the green plane, Mike thought. You wanted one of those rubbish days. Because it might be a plane returning to the airport shortly after take-off, stuffed full of Jet A-1. Because it might be an aircraft with ice in the fuel tanks and its engine gone. Because it might have had a heavy landing and burst ten tyres on its undercarriage, or twenty. Because it could be on fire in one of twenty-six places. And because you had to be ready for anything.

Zoe, Nick and Sky came through security and went to the lounge.

There was a small play area for children. Sky busied herself banging some plastic bricks together while Nick examined the baggage tags on their boarding cards, and checked the passports, and consulted the departure screen for their gate number. And then did it all again.

Zoe swallowed hard. It was happening. It was really happening.

Beyond the high glass windows of the lounge, planes as big as ocean liners queued on the runway: Jumbos and 777s and Airbus 380s all waiting their turn to hurtle from the ground.

'I'll be right back,' Zoe said, and caught the look of

alarm on Nick's face as she turned away and walked out of the lounge.

Near the door there were travellers who had just passed through security. They were collecting their bags, putting their belts on, stuffing keys and coins and phones back in their pockets, slipping laptops into travel bags, reclaiming their dignity and their shoes. Beyond the metal detectors and the security guards there were more people waiting patiently. And beyond a distant wall, Zoe knew, even though she couldn't see her, there was the lady who had checked their passports and boarding cards and told Sky that she was adorable, just adorable.

The traffic is all one way, Zoe thought.

The traffic was all heading towards getting on those planes, as surely as every life heads towards a grave. There was no way out. No escape.

Zoe went to the toilet, aware that her breath was getting shorter.

Closing the door of the stall behind her, she closed the lid of the toilet, sat down and pulled a pack of cigarettes out of her bag. She hadn't smoked for years, and was surprised to see how alarmist the health warnings had become. DIE, DIE, DIE, it said on the side of the packet. YOU ARE DEFINITELY GOING TO DIE. Or perhaps she was just imagining it.

She put one in her mouth, wondering what she should do next.

She struck a match.

She lit the cigarette.

Then Zoe puffed on it nervously, trying to ignore

the wave of nausea as she thought how much she hated smoking.

Do I have to go? she asked herself. Do I really have to go? Even now, can they *make* me go?

If I explain . . .

And then the smoke alarm went off.

'Go,' Mike said, feeling his blood pump as the station's tannoy reported an emergency.

And they went.

Mike led a responding team of five out to the rig. When they answered the call on the fire station's tannoy, they knew nothing about what they were heading towards. It could be anything. And anything was what they trained for, what they steeled themselves for. It was only when they were in the rig and on their way that the airport's central operations room, the Star Centre, filled them in.

There were codes used for certain emergencies. Terrorist activity. Physical assaults. But there was no code for this one.

'Fire in departures, Terminal Five, ladies toilet adjacent to Gordon Ramsay's. Terminal staff attending.'

Mike's driver chuckled, but did not touch the brakes of the rig as they hurtled towards the terminal building. Even if it was next door to nothing, they still had to respond.

'There will always be some idiot sneaking a smoke before they board,' the driver said.

Mike watched the airport flash by, his face set in the hard lines of a man who is trained to risk his life for strangers, and he found that he could not smile with the others.

As if in a dream, the firefighter appeared before Zoe in full firefighting regalia.

He wore a bulky-looking blue suit with flashes of silver and yellow on the jacket and trousers. He had a bright yellow helmet and heavy rubber black boots. He had a sort of utility belt around his waist, such as Batman might approve of, containing a bewildering array of tools. Zoe thought he was like a walking Swiss Army knife. Later, when she thought about the first sight of him standing outside the toilet door, in her imagination she could have sworn that he was carrying a hose. But that wasn't possible, was it?

'Hello,' Mike said to Zoe. 'Have you got a minute?'

'I was scared,' she said. 'That's all.'

'But there's no need to be scared,' he said. Zoe followed Mike out of the toilet. There were four more firemen outside. People were looking and pointing at Zoe. But she saw that Mike was staring up at the Departures board. 'Where you off to?' he asked her.

'Canada,' Zoe said. 'Toronto. The BA flight.'

Mike smiled. 'You've got ages yet,' he said. 'You like getting to the airport early, don't you?'

'Not me,' Zoe said. 'That's my husband. I would be happy to never get here.'

Then Nick and Sky were there, staring at Zoe and the fireman, and wondering what she had done.

'Can you spare her for a while?' Mike asked them.

* * *

10

Zoe rode back to the fire station with them.

On the way they passed the green plane, the fires all out now, and Zoe thought she was seeing things when she noticed that the perimeter of the training ground was covered in smashed cars. Every kind of car in every degree of destruction. Vans and trucks too. On their side and upside down. Smashed up and bashed up and trashed. Windows caved in and engines pulped and roofs flattened.

'We cut them up,' Mike explained, following her gaze. 'To get the people out. And you see that green plane? We set fire to it in twenty-six different ways. That's what we do most of the time.' He glanced at her face. 'Nothing bad is going to happen,' he said. 'I promise you. But if it ever does – we're ready.'

Mike showed her around the fire station. The giant four- and six-wheel rigs. Rows of harnesses, helmets and hoses so infinitely long that they looked as though they could stretch around the world. He showed her all this with a kind of wild pride and she thought of a book she had read at school: Gatsby throwing his shirts on the bed to impress Daisy. Everyone was very friendly. Everything was spotless. It was a world of men waiting for something catastrophic to happen.

'It's very clean,' she said.

Mike looked a bit embarrassed. 'Friday is our wash-up day,' he said. Today was a Friday. 'Perhaps it's not always quite so clean.'

They gave her a cup of tea with lots of sugar and Mike talked all the while, explaining how there are 110 firefighters at Heathrow, with 27 men on a watch

– a twelve-hour shift – and four watches around the clock. One watch on days, one watch on nights, and two at home, resting.

'Which watch are you?' Zoe asked.

'We're green watch,' said Mike.

'Like the plane you set fire to,' she noted.

'Yes,' he said, as though it had never occurred to him before, the way green watch was colour-coordinated with the green plane. 'There's something I want you to see,' he said.

It was the tallest ladder in the world.

Mike called it an ALP – everything was an acronym with the men at the fire station, Zoe realized – and she had to get them to tell her twice that it was an Aerial Ladder Platform before she got it straight in her head.

Then one of the firefighters was helping her into an orange harness, and when that was comfortable she joined Mike on the metal platform of the ALP. He clipped them both to the rail of the platform and the thing, the ALP, began to rise.

It rose above the fire station.

It rose straight up and then it seemed to unfurl itself, and discover another ladder that had been hiding inside it, and rise even higher.

There were the runways down there, Zoe saw – two of them, she noticed for the first time – and there were the planes parked in their stands or taxiing to the runways or rising gracefully into the blue summer sky.

And then, impossibly, the ladder unfurled itself yet again and they were looking down on the roof of

Terminal 5 and the Air Traffic Control tower was at eye-level. They were thirty metres high and still rising on a ladder that was far higher than any ladder on any fire engine in existence.

And for the first time she saw the secret city of the airport. She saw the secret city in all its calm glory, and its unruffled order, and the way everything worked and nothing bad happened. From up there on the fireman's ladder, Zoe looked down at the airport, and she saw a safe world.

Mike was talking all the while. Zoe found that she could tune in and out and get the general gist of it.

'There would be two of us up here and we would have one hundred metres of hose that can unload eleven thousand litres of water in four minutes,' Mike said.

Zoe smiled. 'That's nice, Mike.'

They both looked at the airport. It looked like a place where nothing bad could ever happen. Even high in the sunlit calm, Zoe knew that wasn't quite true. But she also knew that they were ready. And that she was ready too.

'What's in Toronto?' Mike said.

'My parents are out there," Zoe said. "My father – he's not very well. They say – the doctors – that he hasn't got very long. And he's never seen our daughter. So . . .'

She turned away so that he couldn't see her face.

'That's no good,' Mike said. 'That's rotten luck.'

'It's okay,' Zoe said. 'Or at least, it's a lot better now.'

*   *   *

Just before their plane pierced the clouds a man in a window seat gave a strangled gasp.

'A green plane!' he said. 'On the ground! I saw it! A green plane and it was on fire!'

Across the aisle, sitting calmly between her husband and her daughter, Zoe sipped her champagne and smiled to herself.

She felt the plane rise higher.

Two

Fur, Actually

Tim got down on his knees to take a better look at the white lion cub.

It was inside a green crate with a small barred window and even in the cool shadows of the cargo terminal at Heathrow its fur looked as white as bone.

'Hello there,' Tim said softly, smiling with shy delight at the sight of this creature. The white lion cub looked far more like a dog than a cat, a surly pup that now strutted on bandy legs to the front of its crate to bare its fangs at Tim, as if unsure whether it should play with him or rip his face off.

Tim peered at the documents in his hand. He cleared his throat.

'You're going to be staying with us for a while,' he said. 'I know you thought you were going to a zoo in Belgium, but whoever packed your crate in South Africa did a lousy job.'

He looked disapprovingly at the green crate that housed the white lion cub. The air vents were not big enough. There was no real bedding, just a scrap of blanket. And the crate itself was just about the right size for a domestic moggy, but way too small for a white lion cub.

'There are strict regulations about transporting live animals,' Tim said, and the white lion cub cocked its head to one side, as if this was news to him. 'And this shoebox they stuck you in breaks all of them. We're going to contact the airline and give them two days to re-crate you to my satisfaction. After that, you're the Property of the Crown.' The cub showed its teeth and Tim let it have a bit of a chew on his fingers until he could no longer stand the pain. 'Now, how about a saucer of milk back at my place?' he said.

A small blonde woman crouched down beside him and looked into the crate. The white lion cub considered her for a moment and then lifted a front paw, as if to strike.

'What is it?' said Jaswinder 'Jazz' Smith of the UK Border Agency. 'Some kind of exotic dog?'

'It's a lion,' Tim said. 'And it just missed its flight to Belgium. What else you got for me, Jazz?'

'Plenty,' she said.

The pair of them stood up and Jazz leafed through the sheaf of papers in her hand.

'At T5 there's a giant scorpion that crawled into the suitcase of a honeymoon couple coming back from Cancún in Mexico,' she said. 'And there's a white-throated monitor that's been seized by UKBA. Endangered species, right?'

Tim nodded, picturing the lizard with its large muscular body, its strong short legs and thick vicious tail. He would have to watch out for that tail.

'Someone tried to smuggle it in?' he said, wondering how much a white-throated monitor lizard went for on the black market these days.

Jazz shook her head. 'It was in a crate of Golden Delicious from the Cape,' she said.

Tim smiled. 'Nobody wants their organic fruit sprayed with pesticide these days,' he said. 'So we get all sorts of stowaways. That it?'

'Not quite – some nutter came back from Las Vegas with two rattlesnakes in his rucksack,' she said. 'They escaped just as the in-flight entertainment was being switched off for landing. The cleaners are refusing to go on board. I've got some seized rhino horns that may or may not be fake that I want you to take a look at – but they can wait. Everything can wait. The priority is the rattlesnakes on the flight from Vegas.'

'I'll get my pillowcase,' he said. 'It's in the car. They'll be quite happy in my pillowcase.'

'Oh, good,' Jazz said. 'Because that's really what's concerning me, Tim – the happiness of the rattlesnakes.'

Tim took one more look at the white lion cub and then followed Jazz to the exit of the cargo terminal. She paused in the doorway and as he reached her side he saw what she was looking at. A dozen horses were leaving a giant Airbus and being gently led onto three caged lorries by their grooms.

'Beautiful,' Jazz said.

'Yes,' Tim said.

They were polo ponies from Argentina, thoroughbreds crossed with local Criollo horses. Everyone outside the cargo terminal stopped what they were doing for a few

17

seconds to watch the horses being loaded onto the lorries. And they were indeed beautiful.

Although to Tim Brady of the Heathrow Animal Reception Centre, they were no more beautiful than a white lion cub, or a monitor lizard, or a pair of runaway rattlesnakes.

Tim didn't know much about cars, but he knew that the car he pulled his Nissan Micra alongside in the ARC car park was a Porsche. Or perhaps a Ferrari. Or maybe a Maserati.

He looked at it with vague interest as he carried the pillowcase inside.

He could see the man and woman in the waiting area, talking urgently to each other. They were both tall, tanned and wearing dark glasses. From the same privileged world, if not the same generation. The man was perhaps fifteen years older than the woman, who for some reason did not look like any other woman that Tim Brady had ever seen in his life.

One of Tim's colleagues, a girl called Wanda who was wonderful with reptiles, was suddenly in his face, grinning wildly and talking in a mad whisper.

'It's *her*,' Wanda said. 'Don't you recognize her?'

'No,' said Tim.

Wanda waved her hands.

'Can't you see? It's her! She was in that film – what was it? *Jane Eyre*? *Jane Austen*? *Gosford Park*? *Finsbury Park*? Where there's the man and he gets his trousers wet – or is it his shirt? – and then there's the misunderstanding, but they sort it all out. You know.'

18

But he didn't know. He didn't have the faintest idea what Wanda was talking about. He shook his head, absent-mindedly fingering the top of the pillowcase.

'Well, she hasn't got a bonnet on, has she?' Wanda said. 'That's why you don't recognize her. She's not in all the kit.'

Wanda looked over at the glamorous couple – the thin, fabulous young woman, who was apparently famous too, apart from everything else, and the rich-looking, serious-looking older man. Wanda's smile disappeared.

'They've been waiting for you,' she said. 'They're not very happy. About waiting. But you said that you had to be the one who talked to them.'

'I did?'

Wanda nodded. 'It was their dog,' she said. 'The one that died.'

'Ah,' he said, understanding now, handing her the pillowcase. Inside it, life seemed to stir and slither and sigh. '*Crotalus oreganus*,' he said. 'Two of them. Be careful.'

Wanda grinned. 'Rattlesnakes?' she said. 'Cool.'

She took the pillowcase and disappeared.

Tim drew in a deep breath, held it and let it go. But it didn't really make him feel any better. He went through to the waiting area and the couple looked up at him.

'Are you the guy that's going to talk to us?' said the man, standing up. His shirt had perhaps one or possibly two too many buttons undone and Tim could see a small forest of silverish hairs on the man's tanned chest.

'Yes, I am,' Tim said, holding out his hand. 'I'm—'

The man shook his head and laughed, ignoring Tim's hand. Tim slowly withdrew it.

'Cut to the chase, buddy,' the man said. Tim thought that he sounded very American – possibly more American than anyone Tim had ever met in his life. 'What happened to my fiancée's dog?' the man demanded. 'You lose it? Did it wind up in Frankfurt?' He turned to the young woman. 'I *told* you that's the problem,' he said, triumphant. 'I *told* you. These dumb-ass schmucks have lost your dog and now we get their pathetic excuses and lame apologies.'

The young woman took off her sunglasses. She had the bluest eyes that Tim had ever seen and the sight of those eyes gave him a stab of real sadness. This was a terrible thing.

'I'm sorry,' he said, addressing the young woman and not the older man. 'Your dog – Finn, a Golden Retriever, three years old – did not survive the journey from Los Angeles. He died here – this morning – but it was the flight that killed him.'

There was silence in the room.

Somewhere in the distance there was the *clop-clop* sound of horses' hooves.

And then the man erupted.

'Dead?' he said, and the young woman physically recoiled at the word. 'The dog – the dog is dead? Is that what you're telling us, buddy? That the dog is actually *dead*?'

'Yes.' Tim half-shook his head. 'Believe me, I know that this is distressing and shocking news . . .'

The man slumped back in his chair and stared up at Tim in disbelief. The young woman's mouth was open and she seemed to be struggling to breathe.

'You killed the dog,' the man said. 'You killed the dog!'

'Finn,' the young woman said, the sudden flash of anger choked with tears that welled just below the surface. 'His name is – was – Finn. Please stop calling him *the dog*.'

The man was suddenly calm.

'I'm going to sue you, little man,' he said, jabbing a finger at Tim. 'And I am going to sue the airline. And then I am going to sue everybody else. But first – I'm going to sue the damn airline. They flew him across with the cargo, right?' the man demanded. 'Checked him in with the damn cargo as if he was a bag of golf clubs.'

'It is not the fault of the airline,' Tim said. 'They have strict rules about heating, lighting and ventilation for transporting dogs. And they follow them rigorously. That's not the reason why Finn is dead.'

'Who's your boss?' the man said. 'I want to talk to your boss. I'm going to sue him too. Who is the man that runs this joint?'

'That would be me,' Tim said.

'What are you, exactly?' the man said.

'I'm an Animal Health Inspector,' Tim said.

The man laughed harshly.

'Let me tell you, buddy – you're doing a lousy job.'

Tim saw that the blue eyes were upon him.

'Then, if the airlines are so careful, why did Finn die?' she said.

21

Tim saw two things at once. That she was English, despite the mild, mid-Atlantic drawl that had been grafted on top. And that she was holding something.

A worn old dog lead with a silver name-tag. It moved through her long fingers like a rosary.

Tim sat down beside her so that she was now between him and the man. Tim could no longer see the man, only hear him. He appeared to be having a chat with himself.

'I don't believe this,' the man was saying. 'She loved that damn mutt.'

'We get one hundred animals pass through here every day,' Tim told her quietly. He wanted her to understand. He needed her to know. 'Every animal that you can think of, and plenty you can't. Racehorses and cheetahs and Komodo dragons. Poisonous scorpions and domestic pets. Animals that are shipped in and animals that are smuggled in and animals that hide in someone's suitcase or in a crate of fruit. Ten thousand dogs a year. Six thousand cats. Ferrets . . .' He paused, unsure of the latest statistics on ferrets. Then he ploughed on. 'Ferrets galore. Thirty-five million fish. We accept every animal. And this – this now – this with you – what we are doing now – this is the absolute worst part of my job.'

The young woman nodded. 'Okay,' she said. Her face did look familiar. He thought perhaps he had seen it once in a dream. 'But what happened to Finn?'

'Finn was too heavily sedated,' Tim said. 'I'm sure that the vet who sedated him was trying to be kind – trying to spare Finn some of the distress of being transported from Los Angeles to London. But the cargo

22

hold of an aircraft is pressurized at nine thousand feet and what would be a normal dose on land has three times the effect in the air – just as a glass of wine hits you harder on a plane than it does on the ground. It put too great a strain on his heart.'

The man stood up. He was jabbing angrily at some palm-held device and muttering something about a lawyer who was going to enjoy burying a loser like Tim.

'That's it?' the young woman said. 'Just that? It seems – I don't know – such a banal reason for Finn to die.'

'I've seen the handling report from the airline,' Tim said. 'I've checked the travelling container. And I've looked at all the paperwork. Your dog – Finn – was compliant with the pet travel scheme. He was up to date on all his shots, all of that . . .' He looked down at the lead with the silver name-tag. He was not certain that he could look at the blue eyes for much longer. 'You are – if I may say – clearly a loving and responsible owner. And this is a tragedy.' He looked at the eyes for what he thought might be the last time. 'But it's not a mystery,' he said. 'The vet in LA over-sedated . . . Finn.'

The young woman was thinking.

'Where is he now?' she said.

'The vet?' the man said. 'Probably on the golf course. I'm going to sue him, too.'

'*Finn*,' the young woman said.

'He's here,' Tim said. 'Finn is here. And there will be a post-mortem, if you request one. If not, you can take Finn away with you for burial. Or you can leave him here at the Animal Reception Centre.'

The man sneered above his palm-held device. 'And you'll dispose of him, will you?'

Tim didn't look away from the young woman.

'Yes,' he said. 'We will dispose of him. If that is what you want.'

'I want to see him,' she said. 'I want to see Finn. And I want to take him away with me. And I want to give him a proper burial.'

The man was volcanic. 'Jesus Christ! We've got dinner at the Ivy in two hours! We can't take a dead dog with us to the Ivy! What are we meant to do? Check him at the cloakroom with the umbrellas? Are you out of your tiny mind?'

The woman stood up. Tim stood with her. He was surprised that she was so tiny. There was no extra flesh on her face or her body, and it somehow made her seem like a very tall woman. He could understand how a camera could love her at first sight. How anybody could, really.

'Will you please stop talking now, please?' she said to the man. And Tim saw that the lead was shaking in her hands.

The man was suddenly concerned, lavishly conciliatory.

'Honey, do you really think it's a good idea to see, er, Finn? He's gone to dog heaven now, baby, and there's nothing we can do about it.' The phone in his fist began to vibrate and he glanced down at it quickly. 'It's been a long day. You're tired. We have a big dinner ahead. We can't miss our dinner at the Ivy. The dog – old Finn, bless him – would have wanted it this way.'

'I'm going to see Finn now,' she said. 'And you can wait for me here. Or you can go to the big dinner. You can do whatever you want. But what I want is to see my dog.'

She looked at Tim.

'This way,' he said.

She followed him down a short corridor to a small changing room. Blue and green coats hung on hangers with a neat line of rubber boots below them. There was a small sink for scrubbing hands.

'How often does this happen?' she said. 'A dog that dies?'

'It doesn't happen often,' Tim said. 'Dogs seem to get a level of attention that some other animals don't get.' He thought of the white lion cub inside its small, airless green box. 'It doesn't happen very often,' he repeated. 'But it happens.' He pulled a green coat off a hanger. 'We have to put on a coat and wash our hands, and we have to step in that,' he said, indicating a tray on the floor that stunk of some kind of powerful disinfectant. 'The boots are optional,' he said, frowning at her high heels with their red soles. 'You can wear your own shoes if you want, but you'd have to dip them in the tray. It usually depends how expensive your shoes are.'

'These are Christian Louboutin,' she said, glancing down at her shoes and then back at him.

'And are they expensive?' he said.

She stared at him for a moment. 'Give me some boots,' she said.

They washed their hands, pulled on their coats and dabbed the soles of their rubber boots in the tray of disinfectant. Then they went into the ARC proper.

They passed through a door and into a kitchen stacked high with dog and cat food. Then there was a long line of washing machines, all churning away, and plastic baskets full of soiled blankets waiting their turn. She followed him through a doorway and into the open air, past a long line of high cages, all empty and silent.

'The bird section,' he said. 'Regulations are so strict these days that we don't get a lot of visitors in the bird section.'

Then they passed through another door and back inside, and here were the dogs. They were a fine-looking collection of dogs – pure bred, deeply loved, well-travelled dogs of the world. Labradors and Dalmatians and German shepherds, Great Danes and Akitas and Afghan hounds, all of them in their own spacious cages, which opened up at the back into a small, open-air yard. They looked pampered and proud.

'Finn's in here,' Tim said.

He took her into one of the cages and there was Finn. He looked as if he was sleeping, Tim thought. Finn didn't look the way his father had looked when he saw him for the last time in hospital, wearing an expression in death that he had never once worn in life. Finn wasn't like that; he looked genuinely at peace.

Somebody had wrapped a blanket around him, as if to keep him warm.

The young woman sat down beside her dog and stroked him. After a while she looked up at Tim and smiled.

'He was loved, you know,' she said. 'It's not just all those other dogs out there. My dog was loved, too.'

Tim nodded. 'I know,' he said. 'I know you loved him. This is not your fault. It's not because you didn't love him enough.'

'When we were on the plane, I thought I heard him,' the young woman said. 'I thought I heard the cry of a dog in the hold. My dog. Finn.'

'I've heard of that before,' Tim said gently. 'But I don't think it's possible. To hear a dog in the hold. Perhaps I'm wrong.'

He left her alone, telling her that she could find him in the next section along when she was ready. Glancing back, he glimpsed her bent over the golden retriever, still stroking it, still holding the lead with the silver name-tag, and mouthing words that nothing living could hear.

Fifteen minutes later he felt her standing by his side as he looked at a dozen small pointed faces that pressed their snouts through the bars of their cage and stared back at him with reflective yellow eyes ringed with black fur. They had bushy tails in black-and-white stripes and their wild chatter sounded like mad birds.

'Lemurs?' she said.

He looked at her, impressed. 'Yes,' he said. 'Lemurs. They think I've got some grapes. They all love grapes.

27

You love grapes, don't you? They were seized,' he told her. 'I want them rehoused together. I don't want to split up a social group.'

'Are you a vet?' she said.

'No,' he said. 'I just take care of the animals that come through the airport. Are you an actress?'

She shook her head. 'I was a model and then I did some acting,' she said. 'I was in something that did quite well. But I'm not an actress. Not yet. I'm taking lessons. Look – I want to see where he died. Will you show me round?'

It was like being in a private zoo.

She saw giant anteaters and poison dart frogs and Komodo dragons. He showed her four dwarf crocodiles that had been destined for a private swimming pool in Putney. Wallabies that had been seized en route from Indonesia to a dealer in Eastern Europe. An Egyptian sand boa constrictor that was heading to a pet shop that had gone bankrupt in Birmingham.

She saw a cheetah bound for Sweden that had torn his mouth on a sharp edge of his crate and been seized by the UK Border Agency. A swaggering capuchin monkey with a baby-pink face that had been discovered in cargo when the police were searching for a bomb. Glass cases containing scorpions that had stowed away in fruit containers from every lush, tropical corner of the planet. She saw hundreds of soft-shell turtles basking under warm lamps and feeding on water full of bloodworms. And a *Caiman crocodilus* that lunged for her hand and made her gasp out loud.

'Careful,' Tim said. 'He'll eat anything he can get into his mouth. Including your finger.'

He took her outside. A white moon hung in a pale blue sky above the airport.

The horses were already leaving the ARC's stables. They watched them for a while, as the grooms carefully led them to the lorries that would take them away from the ARC to a polo ground south of London.

Next to the stables there were containers. Neat piles of boxes, crates and cages for every kind of living creature. She was staring up at one of them and he followed her gaze. *Hi, my name is Finn*, it said on the front.

'He was a really good dog,' she said, unable to take her eyes from the crate just yet. 'Some people don't get it. How a dog can mean that much. As much as a human. That this is a real bereavement. My boyfriend doesn't get it.'

'I get it,' he said.

Then she looked at him. 'I know you do,' she said. 'I don't want to take Finn away with me. I want him to stay here. With you. If that's all right.'

'Whatever you want is good,' he said.

She held out the worn old dog lead with its silver name-tag. He took it from her and held it carefully, as if it was something that could be easily broken.

They stared at each other for a while.

'So is that it?' she said quietly.

Tim's face lit up.

'Apart from the snakes,' he said.

He had a special tool for digging out the snakes.

A wooden stick with a metal hook on the end. He showed it to her with a kind of bashful pride as they stood before a shelf full of glass cases stuffed with vegetation.

'They can't get away from it, but that doesn't mean they like it,' he said, fishing a particularly evil-looking snake from its leafy box.

The snake curled around the wood and around Tim's hand, hissing like a punctured tyre as it lifted its flat head to study him. It was somewhere between orange and red with white, black-etched rings between each bar of colour.

'I hope you don't mind snakes,' he said. 'I know some people don't like them very much.'

She could hardly breathe. 'I guess I don't mind them,' she said.

'Are you going to whip me?' he said.

'What?' she said.

'I was talking to the snake.'

'Oh.'

'This is just a milk snake,' he said. 'Completely harmless. You're harmless, aren't you?' The snake hissed at him. 'But the milk snake mimics the coral snake,' he said. 'It looks identical. So that, if a predator comes along and sees it, it thinks it's highly venomous.'

'But it's not the real thing,' she said, daring to move a little closer.

'No,' he said. 'It's not the real thing.'

She moved closer still.

'But how do you know the real thing when you see it?' she said. 'When you finally see the real thing for the first time in your life? How do you know?'

He looked thoughtful. 'I guess you know it when you see it,' he said.

She was right by his side now.

'I'm meant to be getting married,' she said.

'That's good, isn't it?' he said.

'No,' she said. 'It's a bloody joke.'

Tim did not know what to say. So he turned to the snake, cooing with amused affection as it lifted its vicious head. Then his face grew serious.

'But I can understand why your boyfriend is angry,' he said.

At first she did not reply. With those luminous blue eyes that were adored by millions, she watched this man who had a red milk snake wrapped around one hand and a worn old leather dog lead with a silver name-tag in the other.

She moved even closer.

Tim and the red milk snake both looked at her.

'He's not my boyfriend,' she said.

Three

The Pilot's Room

The pilot had seen things that most men will never see.

Once, halfway across the Atlantic, flying a 777 at 35,000 feet, he saw a blood-red moon rise into a black sky and for a moment he could not breathe – it was as if there was nothing else in the universe, just the red moon in the black sky and his aircraft.

And once, flying east to west, unravelling time, he had seen the double sunrise – watched the sun rise twice on the same day – and it was as if he was not travelling high above the Indian Ocean but through time itself.

And once he had been flying in the high latitudes when the sky erupted around him into a swirl of green, blue and white, and he was not looking at the Northern Lights, he was inside them.

It was difficult to explain the wonders he had witnessed. The pilot had taken photographs of these earthly miracles but it was not the same as being there. It could never be the same. So in the end he stopped talking about it, and he stopped taking photographs, and he stopped trying to explain the beauty and the mystery of all he had seen.

Because only another pilot would really understand.

The pilot woke before dawn while his family were still sleeping.

After a month on standby, waiting in vain for the call to take the place of a scheduled pilot, he realized he was hungry to fly again. He shaved, showered, and decided that breakfast could wait until he was at the airport. Then he got his bicycle out of the shed and wheeled it down the drive.

Outside the house next door, a fat man in a suit and tie was standing next to his car, watching the pilot with an amused grin. This was the pilot's next-door neighbour, George, who was always tickled to see the pilot getting on his bicycle. George licked his index finger and pretended to gauge the direction of the wind.

'Good tailwind today, Captain? Careful – we are expecting some turbulence around the Hanger Lane gyratory. Please keep your bicycle clips on at all times during the journey.'

The pilot smiled politely, the sound of George's laughter ringing around inside his bicycle helmet. The pilot had shown George his photographs when he had first moved in. The blood-red moon in the pitch-black sky. The double sunrise. The Northern Lights.

But George was something in the City. And there was no way that he could really understand.

*   *   *

The pilot strolled through the airport.

He was dressed to fly – white shirt, blue tie and the silver wings on his blue, double-breasted jacket. The jacket had three stripes on the sleeves because the pilot was a Senior First Officer. On his head he wore a peaked cap that contained an important document – the pilot's roster for the month. The hat might look as if it was for show, but it contained the pilot's immediate future. Also in there, under the roster, was a photograph of his wife and their small son.

It was the start of the summer months and Terminal 5 Departures was at its busiest. The pilot did not notice the old man until he was standing right in front of him.

The old man did not look as though he was flying anywhere today. He looked as though he was lost, and had been lost for many years. He was very thin, unshaven, and when he smiled at the pilot, he revealed teeth like broken tombstones. His smell was strong – like a broken bottle of wine on a dirty pavement. That was what the pilot noticed most of all. The smell of the old man.

The pilot nodded briskly and stepped to the side, trying to go around the old man. But the old man moved with him, surprisingly nimble for someone who smelled like a smashed case of Sauvignon Blanc. The old man nodded in sly recognition at the silver wings on the pilot's chest, and then he looked the pilot in the eye.

'*Oh, I have slipped the surly bonds of earth, and danced the skies on laughter-silvered wings,*' said the old man, his voice like a dead body dragged across gravel. '*Put out my hand and touched the face of God.*'

The pilot stared in disbelief at the old man.

'What?' he said. 'What do you mean?'

It was as if someone had seen the red moon rise in the black sky, or watched the double sunrise, or flown through the Northern Lights. It was as if some unmet stranger, some unknown brother, had seen all of these things with the pilot, and understood.

Then the police were there. Two of them. An inspector and a sergeant. The police at Heathrow are the most heavily armed in the country and both the inspector and the sergeant carried Heckler & Koch MP5 submachine guns, Glock handguns, handcuffs, Taser guns and extendable telescopic truncheons. But they smiled at the old man with infinite kindness.

'Come on, dad,' the sergeant gently chided. 'Don't bother the nice young pilot.'

'Now we've talked to you about harassing the pilots, haven't we, dad?' said the inspector.

The old man looked desperate. And secretly angry.

'I wasn't harassing him,' he said. 'And I do not believe I am your father.'

The policemen chuckled good-naturedly. The old man glanced swiftly at the pilot and began to edge away.

'Wait a minute,' the pilot said. 'What did you say? What are those words? What do you mean?' But the old man was already melting into the crowds, so he turned to the policemen. 'What did he say to me?' the pilot said.

35

But they did not answer the pilot. They were wondering what they should do about the old man.

'Poor old boy,' said the sergeant.

'Yes,' agreed the inspector. 'They say he used to be a pilot.'

The sergeant nodded. 'That's right, and I used to be Hugh Hefner,' he said. 'Horrible it was – all those Bunnies up at the Playboy Mansion. They wouldn't leave me alone.'

Their Heckler & Koch submachine guns jiggled with their laughter. Then the inspector looked serious.

'I don't want to get a court order out on him, but I will if he keeps this up,' he said. 'He's loitering at the airport for no valid reason. And that's not allowed.'

'You want me to call Outreach?' the sergeant asked.

The inspector shook his head. 'The old man's not homeless,' he said. 'He just loves being at the airport.'

'What was all that about?' the pilot said. 'What did he mean? "*Danced the skies on laughter-silvered wings . . .*"'

But the old man was gone. And the two policemen didn't know what he was talking about. They began to wander away.

And the pilot knew that his question was pointless.

Because he knew exactly what the old man had meant.

The pilot's hat was endlessly useful.

Not only did he keep his flying roster in the lining but the deep interior was perfect for storing his belongings when he passed through the special security area for flight crew located on the far side of BA's first-class check-in desks. The pilot would have been lost without his hat.

Beyond security, he went immediately to the crew report centre, found a vacant computer and swiped in with his ID card.

The screen confirmed that the pilot was flying to Paris today and that he would be staying over – the first of the ten nights he would spend away from home this month. He discovered which of the airline's 350 captains he would be flying with and smiled at the name that appeared. They had flown together twice before and the pilot had appreciated the older man's calm wisdom and flying experience. It was always good to get on with your captain, the pilot thought. After all, they were going to be locked behind a bulletproof door together for several hours.

The pilot looked at the flight plan, checked the weather and printed out the flight map. He walked down to the room where the flight crew were meeting and, when it was time, together they all walked through the terminal to the gate.

The sun shone bone-white on the nose of their aircraft as they loaded six tons of Jet A-1 aviation fuel.

The pilot went back to the cabin to look at the fifty Elvis impersonators they were carrying. The sight made him smile.

And then, five minutes ahead of schedule, they slipped the surly bonds of earth.

*   *   *

The airport never really slept, the pilot thought. It only closed its eyes, and waited for the dawn.

It was late when he arrived back at Terminal 5. So late that there would be no more flights until the early arrivals from East Asia started landing just before dawn.

But there were people sleeping at the terminal, suit-cases by their side, rucksacks for a pillow. They all looked as though they were too late or too early for their flight, although the pilot knew that the police always watched for fake travellers – people who preferred sleeping inside the climate-controlled Richard Rogers architecture rather than on the streets of the city.

And the old man was there, as the pilot somehow knew he would be. They stood looking at each other for a while, and it was the pilot who spoke first.

'It's a poem,' he said. 'I went to the English bookstore on the Rue de Rivoli. They didn't have it for sale, but I found that much out.' He shrugged. 'All I know is his name.'

The old man nodded. 'John Gillespie Magee, Junior,' he said. 'Born 1922. Died 1941.'

The pilot was stunned. 'Dead at nineteen? And he wrote like that? How is that even possible?'

The old man revealed his ruined teeth. 'The war, you see,' he said.

Then the two policemen were there. The inspector and the sergeant, smiling kindly above their weapons.

'Is everything lovely here?' the sergeant said.

The old man looked at them with a flash of fear. But the pilot nodded.

'We're all right,' he said. 'Everything's fine, officer.'

The policemen went on their way, treading softly as they moved among the weary travellers, and tenderly cradling their Heckler & Koch submachine guns as if they were babes in arms.

In the empty bar of an airport hotel, there were three stories told that night.

First the pilot told the story of how it had begun for him. How he had grown up on the border of the East End and Essex, under the flight path to Heathrow, and it had felt like he had spent his entire childhood looking up at the skies. But he was part of what they called the unlucky generation – the would-be pilots who came of age after 9/11, when the business was shrinking. He found a job as a mechanical engineer at Ford.

But he kept seeing the planes.

He had lessons at Stapleford Aerodrome. He went to Prestwick Flying School. And he found that he had an aptitude for it – like driving a car in 3D, was how he thought of flying – and so he had invested £100,000 of borrowed money in himself, and his dream. Then there was the private pilot's licence, and the job with a small Irish airline, and finally the Holy Grail – a job advertised on the British Airways website, and a successful interview.

'What do you fly?' the old man asked, sipping coffee but smelling of wine.

'Triples,' the pilot said.

'Boeing 777s . . .' The old man smiled, and his watery

eyes got a faraway look. 'Beautiful aircraft. Large engines, long body, low-hanging landing gear.'

'That's the one,' the pilot said.

'First commercial aircraft designed by a computer,' the old man said. 'Triples, eh? They would have been nice.'

Then the old man told his story. It was a story of a broken marriage, a broken family and a broken man. And it was a story of how flying and alcohol will never mix. The old man maintained that his drinking had never endangered anyone and he had suffered a great injustice when he lost his licence.

The pilot nodded, although he had no idea how much of the old man's story was true. But he was sure of this: the old man had once been a pilot.

And finally the old man told the story of John Gillespie Magee, Junior, who on 3rd September 1941 wrote a poem after taking his Spitfire up to 30,000 feet. Magee had scribbled the poem on the back of a letter to his parents, an American father and an English mother. He was killed in his Spitfire two months later.

'John was a pilot,' the old man said. 'But you guessed that much.'

'Of course.'

'Like us,' the old man said.

The bar was empty now. Even the airport was silent. The old man held his breath, waiting for the younger man's answer.

'Yes,' the pilot agreed finally. 'Just like us.'

His wife was still awake when he got home from the Paris run. She went online and found the poem immediately. She read it and told him that it was beautiful. 'High in the sunlit silence,' she said. 'Just like you.' He hugged her and laughed out loud and told her how happy he was to be home. And he told her that she was beautiful, too.

His wife printed the poem out for him before his next run. And from that day on, like so many things that were important to him – the roster of his next flights, the picture of his family and the keys to his front door when he was passing through security – the pilot kept the poem inside his cap.

High Flight

Oh! I have slipped the surly bonds of Earth
And danced the skies on laughter-silvered wings;
Sunward I've climbed, and joined the tumbling mirth
Of sun-split clouds – and done a hundred things
You have not dreamed of – wheeled and soared and
    swung
High in the sunlit silence. Hovering there,
I've chased the shouting wind along, and flung
My eager craft through footless halls of air.
Up, up the long, delirious, burning blue
I've topped the wind-swept heights with easy grace
Where never lark, or ever eagle flew—
And, while with silent, lifting mind I've trod
The high, untrespassed sanctity of space,
Put out my hand and touched the face of God.

John Gillespie Magee, Junior

He never saw the old man again.

Months later, he was told by one of the policemen that airport security had found the old man unconscious in a stairwell, and he had died on the way to hospital. The pilot went to see the stairwell for himself. It overlooked the north runway.

The pilot stood there for quite a while.

It was a good place to watch the planes.

Four

Say Hello, Wave Goodbye

The young woman in the white wedding dress entered the Arrivals hall, still looking radiant after the twelve-hour flight from Seoul, South Korea.

Even with three long-haul flights landing at almost exactly the same time, delivering just under one thousand passengers who would all have to present their travel documents to one of twenty immigration officers, somehow Jaswinder 'Jazz' Smith of the UK Border Agency knew that she would be the one to examine the smiling bride's passport.

Jazz always got the nutters.

Thirty minutes later, with the queues thinning out, Jazz said, 'Next,' and the bride stood before her, holding out the dark green passport of the Republic of Korea.

'This is probably a really stupid question,' Jazz said, taking the passport. 'But what's the purpose of your visit to the UK?'

The girl's smile grew broader. It wasn't just the wedding dress, Jazz thought. She was beautiful.

'I'm getting married,' she said, looking over her shoulder and acknowledging with a graceful nod the smattering of applause in the Non-EU Nationals queue.

'Congratulations,' Jazz said. It was a biometric passport and she deftly read the microchip, which contained details about the passport holder's face – the distance between eyes, ears, nose and mouth. As she had ten thousand times before, Jazz checked these details against the passport photo and the face in front of her.

'To Prince Harry,' the bride said.

Jazz shut the passport but did not hand it back. 'What?' she said.

'I'm getting married to Prince Harry,' the girl said.

Jazz made further checks.

Had the girl in the wedding dress ever been refused entry to the UK? Did she have a return ticket? Did she have sufficient funds for what was planned to be a two-week stay? Had she ever been deported? Had she ever been refused a visa? Was there any incriminating data on file? Was there any possibility that she wasn't really going to get married to Prince Harry?

In the end, Jazz handed back the dark green passport with a smile.

'Enjoy your big day,' she said, and the young woman in the white wedding dress entered the UK.

The officer at the next desk, a middle-aged woman who looked Indian but sounded pure Cockney, glanced over at Jazz.

'I remember when it was Prince Charles they all came over to marry,' she said.

Jazz laughed. 'Before my time,' she said.

*   *   *

More travellers poured into the Arrivals hall. Jazz looked down at the flight lists, the numbers of passengers, and their nationalities. The Americans are coming, she thought.

'Next.'

The man was perhaps forty. He was standing right over the desk and Jazz had to ask him to step back to the line, which he did with a shy apology. But he looked normal – or as normal as anyone looks after travelling from one side of the planet to the other in half a day.

'Purpose of visit?' Jazz asked.

The man took a breath.

'Barack Obama has planted a microchip in my brain and he is currently streaming live images to my frontal lobes,' the man said. 'So I am here to claim political asylum.'

Jazz and the man – Donald Harrison, it said in his passport – stared at each other for a bit. Funnily enough, Jazz had heard this one before.

'And I want to see *We Will Rock You*,' Donald Harrison said. 'The Freddie Mercury musical? Freddie Mercury of Queen?'

'I've seen it, sir,' Jazz said, her voice flat and hard. She indicated a small corral of seats next to the passport control desks – the Not-OK Corral, Jazz called it. 'I am going to ask you to take a seat, sir.'

His eyes were bright with the news that Jazz had seen *We Will Rock You*.

'Any good?' he asked.

'I'm not really a Queen fan,' Jazz confessed. 'My

husband likes Queen. I got tickets for his birthday. Take a seat, will you, please?'

Donald Harrison snorted. 'You don't like Queen?' said the man with President Obama's microchip in his brain. 'You must be mad.'

Jazz swiftly processed twenty assorted visitors to the UK. Tourists and businessmen, families and students, young and old and everything in between.

Jazz liked to say that it wasn't her job to refuse entry to the UK. It was her job to have an inner alarm bell – rather like one of those microchips that President Obama plants in people's brains. And when someone wasn't coming to the UK for the right reasons, it was her job to hear that bell ring.

'Next!'

The inner alarm bell rang loud and long when she looked at the passport photo of the young man dressed in black T-shirt, jeans and cowboy boots.

She looked at him and she looked at the passport and she read the biometric data on the microchip and somehow it did not fit. In the passport photo the man looked as though he had had some kind of cosmetic surgery. But in the flesh, he just looked unwell.

'Take a seat,' she said.

They looked at each other and she watched him work out that it was pointless to argue. The man in black joined Donald Harrison in the Not-OK Corral. Jazz looked down at his passport photo again. She was not an expert in forged passports. But she knew a man who was.

'Next!'

An American girl, maybe eighteen, sweet and blonde and pretty. And she wouldn't look Jazz in the eye. And she shifted her weight from foot to foot. And she was so nervous that she almost rattled.

'How long are you planning to stay, Megan?'

'Two weeks,' the girl said quickly. 'Just two weeks. Just two weeks and then I'll – you know – go home.'

Jazz smiled pleasantly. 'And what are you planning to do in the UK?'

'I want to see the wax museum?'

Jazz nodded. Madame Tussauds was a legitimate reason to visit the United Kingdom. Lifelike effigies of Nelson Mandela and Brad Pitt – how could anyone resist?

'What do you want to see there?' Jazz said.

Megan had not been anticipating a follow-up question about the world-famous wax museum.

'Candles?' she offered.

Jazz looked at the young traveller. This girl should not be a problem, Jazz thought.

But she is . . .

'And I want to try some of that world-famous British pizza,' Megan said, and Jazz got that cold, tense feeling that came upon her when she knew that someone was telling her lies.

Jazz had jotted the girl's answers down on the back of her landing card. The information would be stored forever. The fact that she wanted to go to the most famous wax museum in the world to look at the candles. The fact that she could not wait to try the finest pizza that British cuisine could offer. It was all carved in stone now.

Jazz wished that the girl would do herself a favour and stop talking. Because every time she opened her mouth she made it more difficult for Jazz to allow her entry into the United Kingdom.

'May I see your return ticket, Megan?'

But she did not have one.

And that clinched it.

'I'm going to ask you to take a seat, Megan,' Jazz said. 'And I'll be with you shortly.'

At last the girl looked Jazz in the eye, and she seemed to size her up. And what the American girl saw was a small blonde woman, ten years older than herself, and dressed in a blue skirt and a white shirt with the UKBA flash. Her pretty face twisted with a kind of sneering contempt.

'But what about the crazy lady in the wedding dress?' the girl said. 'You let her in.'

Jaswinder Smith of the UK Border Agency took a deep breath.

'Because I don't care if someone lies to themselves,' said Jazz. 'But I don't like it much when they lie to me.'

'This passport is a fake,' said the UKBA officer who knew about these things. 'It's a pretty good fake, although I wouldn't rate it any higher than that.'

Ken was the UKBA officer you went to with what they called 'questioned documents'. He worked mole-like in a small, windowless room off of the UKBA's main office, which was one level up from the Arrivals hall and hidden behind a bank of smoked glass.

Out in the main office space, officers monitored CCTV images of the airport and checked flight lists on their computer screens and watched the passengers in the queues for passport control. Everything was bustle, light and a never-ending parade of planes and people. But Ken's dark little room was the exact opposite. There was nothing in there apart from Ken, a machine called a VSC40, and hundreds of passports from every country on the planet.

There were passports that had been stolen, forged and borrowed. There were expired passports that had been tampered with to make them appear valid. There were passports with pages removed and inserted, passports with photographs that had been changed, altered or substituted, passports with real visa stamps removed and bogus stamps inserted. Ken and his VSC40 saw through them all.

'Nothing feels right about this guy,' Jazz said. 'What do you think?'

Ken adjusted the machine. The VSC40 could read microchips, assess paper quality and read surface features such as visa stamps. It knew its way around watermarks, metallic strips and ink quality. It was a lie detector for passports.

'He makes me think that the ex-KGB guys do the best forgeries,' Ken said, making an adjustment so that he could zoom in on the passport's photograph. 'We see the best forgeries in the world at this airport. What we have here is not in that league.'

He removed the passport and handed it to Jazz. 'Pages have been removed and replaced,' he said. 'Probably some visa stamps he didn't want anyone to see. So they've had to hand-stitch the pages, rethreading the document in the existing holes – there's no high-tech way to do that. It's old school, but it's been done well. They've done minimum damage to the passport and that's always the smart move. But it's the photograph where they give themselves away.'

Jazz looked at the photograph of the man in black. 'Looks weird,' she said.

'Because that's not him,' Ken laughed. 'It's someone else. Look at the area around the mouth and eyes. Hold it horizontally. Can you see the abrasion?'

Jazz held the passport sideways and squinted hard. And she suddenly saw the faintest of scuffmarks on the photograph of the man in black – just a few grey dots, nothing more. But it was there all right. Again she felt the flash of ice-cold irritation that came when she knew she was being deceived.

'So it's some other guy and it has been altered to look like our boy downstairs?' Jazz said.

Ken nodded. 'It does less damage to a passport than a fake photo.' His smile lit up the dark little room. 'It's not a bad idea – if you get away with it.'

Jazz closed the passport. 'Thanks, Ken.'

'You think he's importing controlled substances,' he said.

'I'm thinking that – right here, right now – he has swallowed more cocaine in condoms than you have had hot dinners,' she said.

'One problem with that theory,' Ken said. 'Drug mules very rarely go to the trouble of forging passports. The dealers can always find gullible mugs to carry the product in their gut, working on the business model that enough of them will get through. How do you explain that?'

Jazz shook her head. 'I can't,' she said. 'Yet. Maybe he got ripped off by a mule and is into DIY.'

A young UKBA officer appeared in the doorway. Jazz looked up at him and gave him leave to speak with an imperceptible nod.

'You have three for the holding rooms,' the young man said. 'The American girl – she's making a bit of a fuss. She was shouting about seeing a lawyer. You might want to see her first.'

'No,' Jazz said. 'First we have to catch a plane.'

They walked to the gate just as the aircraft was arriving. Jazz and the young officer – Norm – stood just behind the men from Airside Ops who would tell the flight attendants that they were clear to open the door. And Jazz noticed that Norm was shaking with nerves.

'You've been working mostly Customs, right?' she said.

He nodded. 'We had a mental morning,' he said. 'At Departures we found this guy with twenty grand in cash in the lining of his hand luggage, flying to Istanbul.' Norm smiled, wiping the palms of his hands on his trousers. 'He said it was for safekeeping.'

'Well, you can't be too careful,' Jazz said. 'There are a lot of dodgy characters about these days.'

'You think he was going to buy drugs at source?'

'Maybe. Or he might have been laundering money made over here. Or he could have been off to buy something really expensive – like people. They cost quite a bit. So you gave him the option to leave the money or go before a magistrate and argue his case?'

Norm nodded. 'He said – *I fly.*'

'The smart move.'

'And at Arrivals there was this guy from Dubai with a collection of camel-fighting DVDs. What kind of sicko wants to watch camels fighting? And there was a woman from Vilnius with five thousand cigarettes in her suitcase.'

'She's really got to try cutting down. Norm? Will you do something for me? Try taking a deep breath, will you?'

'And there was this old man from Ghana who wanted to bring in some dead rats on a stick.'

'It's a West African voodoo thing,' she said. 'Each to his own. Listen – calm down a bit, will you? You're babbling, Norm. Is this your first coded landing?'

'Yes.' He wiped the palms of his hands on his trousers again. 'Yes, it is, Officer Smith.'

'It's going to be fine,' Jazz said. 'The man we're meeting is an Iraqi national who has been granted asylum in Greece. But he doesn't want to live in Greece. He wants to live here. So he keeps coming to the UK and pretending to be someone he's not. We have to grab him as soon as he appears, okay? Guys like this, they either leave their passports on the plane or destroy them in the first toilet on land. We're not going to let him get that far. Got it?'

'Got it.'

'Good. Here we go.'

The door opened and the passengers surged out of the plane. Jazz saw a flight attendant with a look of horror on her face and she followed her eyes to a curly-haired man in his twenties who was ripping up his passport and stuffing it into his mouth.

'Oh, this one's good,' Jazz said. 'Oh, this one's very good.'

Jazz and Norm grabbed his arms as he came off the plane and, while he coughed and retched and ingested the last morsels of his Greek passport, they steered him towards the Arrivals hall.

'How's Greece these days?' Jazz said.

'I was never in Greece,' the man croaked, before sagging in their arms and beginning to gag. 'I am from Afghanistan,' he choked. 'Where I was cruelly molested by the Taliban.'

'He's going to be sick,' Norm predicted.

They were outside a men's toilet. Jazz thought about it for a second and then shoved the pair of them towards the entrance.

'Just don't let him out of your sight,' she said.

Norm and the passport-muncher disappeared inside the toilet as a familiar figure walked slowly past her, taking his time, his progress hampered by the arriving passengers flooding in the opposite direction towards the Arrivals hall.

'Donald?' she called. 'Hey, Donald!'

She caught up with him. He looked at her mildly, slightly bewildered, as if they had never met.

'Don't go anywhere, Donald,' Jazz said. 'We need to have a chat. Okay?'

He smiled and they walked back towards Arrivals together. Norm was standing outside the toilet.

Alone.

'I don't know what happened,' he said. 'I washed my hands –'

'Look after Donald,' she said.

Jazz headed back towards the gate, guessing that the man would try to land himself – meaning arrive at one terminal and then attempt to clear Immigration at another. They didn't get many runners. Maybe one a year. There was nowhere to run to.

Sooner or later, Jazz thought, you bang your head up against my border.

She saw him at the end of a long, deserted hall, one of those seemingly infinite empty spaces that could suddenly open up at the airport, and she broke into a run, catching up with him as he paused at a glass wall with the runway beyond, considering his next move.

They looked at each other.

He was a foot taller and twice her weight.

Jazz moved slowly towards him.

'Don't make me take you down,' she said quietly.

He laughed at that, but when he tried to push past her she slipped one leg behind him and shoved his chest hard with the palms of her hands. He fell backwards and went down fast and heavy. She left him there, flat on his back, moaning something about knowing his human rights and being molested by the Taliban while she picked up his holdall and began to search through it for travel documents. But it looked like they had all been eaten.

He jumped up and tried to snatch the holdall from her.

'My bag, my bag!' he cried. 'You give me my bag back!'

'Hey,' she said, frowning as she held it away from him. 'Manners. What's the magic word?'

His face got a sly look.

He wiped a crumb of passport from his bottom lip.

'Asylum,' he said. 'The magic word is . . . asylum.'

Once you cleared passport control you turned left to collect your baggage and get on with your life. But if for some reason you did not clear passport control then you turned right and were escorted beyond a sign saying AUTHORIZED STAFF ONLY to a strip of locked, glass-walled holding rooms.

One of the rooms was for families, stuffed full of brightly coloured, ancient toys. Right now it held a weary-looking man and woman and a tiny child who was contemplating a stuffed monkey with many miles on the clock. The other rooms held Megan, Donald and the man in black.

Jazz looked at them through the glass. The man in black, hunched in his seat, sweating heavily. Donald staring into space, humming a selection of Queen's greatest hits. And Megan, looking at Jazz through the glass, not afraid to meet her eye now as she mouthed one word.

Bitch.

'I'll start with her,' Jazz said, and she swiped the card that let her into the holding room.

'You can't keep me here like this,' Megan said.

'I can keep you here for twenty-four hours,' Jazz said. 'But I don't need that long. May I look in your rucksack?'

There was so much intelligence to be found in bags. Megan threw it at her.

The first thing that Jazz found was a card. Some kind of greetings card. She took it out of the envelope and read, *Good Luck With Your New Life.*

It had been signed inside by lots of people – the kind of card you get when you are going away forever. Some of them seemed to think that they would never be seeing Megan again.

'Do you have a boyfriend here, Megan?' Jazz said, holding up the card. 'Maybe someone you met in the States? Someone you are very fond of? A British guy who you are planning to live with in the UK? Stop me if I'm getting warm.'

'You can't talk to me like that,' Megan said, her face flushing red. 'It's nothing to do with you.'

'I have police powers,' Jazz said. 'I can arrest you, and I can charge you, and if you are found guilty of an offence serious enough, somebody can send you to prison. And I can instruct the airline that brought you in to take you back.'

'And what if they refuse?'

'They never do.'

Megan sat down and covered her face in her hands. 'Ever been in love?' she said.

'Once,' Jazz said.

'And do you know what it's like when you will do anything for him? Absolutely anything?'

'Well,' Jazz said. 'He did talk me into seeing *We Will Rock You*.'

The man in black stood there with sweat pouring down his face, his arms rigid by his side, focusing every fibre of his being on trying not to shake.

He had been removed from the holding area and they were now standing in a bare red-and-grey room.

'This is what is going to happen,' Jazz said. 'I can go to my line manager and ask for permission to give you either a rub down, a strip search or an intimate search. Guess which one I'm going to ask for?' She nodded at Norm. 'It's same sex for searching, so I will not have the pleasure. Have you done your nails, Norm?'

Jazz was holding a piece of cloth that might have been used to clean spectacles. She showed it to the man in black and dabbed it against his forehand.

'This goes into a machine called an Ionscan,' she said. 'It tells me if you have been anywhere near narcotics. Now you might think you've been very careful, but I can promise you that you haven't been careful enough. I shall swab your shoes, your hands, and your perspiration. It is impossible to avoid being contaminated in some way. And when we leave the airport for the detention centre, you will leave in handcuffs, and will have made the transition from passenger to prisoner.'

The man in black stared at her, eyes bulging, grinding his teeth.

'Grand tour first?' Jazz said.

They led him through to a giant X-ray machine. It looked like the kind of metal detector you get at security, but blown up to epic proportions.

'This will show up your intestines and bowels a treat,' Jazz said. 'Then the results go to a radiographer at St Bart's Hospital, who gets back to us in two or three hours.'

The man in black began to tremble. Norm looked nervously at Jazz. She put her face close to the man's ear.

'Ask yourself this,' Jazz said quietly. 'Do I really have two or three hours?'

Finally she showed him the special toilet. This always gave them pause for thought. It looked more like a medieval gallows than a lavatory. There were steep metal steps leading up to a metal platform that seemed sturdy enough to support a scaffold. But instead of a gibbet there was a toilet bowl with no lid. Directly below it there was a steel-framed glass window with two long black rubber gloves built into it, reaching inside like curious snakes.

'This is where it gets messy,' Jazz said. 'You've got – what? Seventy to one hundred sealed wrappers inside you? I've seen people who have swallowed narcotics wrapped inside tin foil and clingfilm wrappers. Can you believe that? You wouldn't be that stupid, would you? Even condoms – well, that violates all sorts of health and safety rules, and it's still a risky business.

Because sometimes they break. Any idea what that does to the human heart?'

He swallowed hard.

'We're both professionals,' he muttered.

'Not you,' Jazz said. 'You're an amateur. This is what I do for a living. Now – before we begin – is there anything you want to tell me?'

The man in black stared at her, eyes wild and bulging. With an enormous effort, he shook his head. He could no longer hold his hands still by his side. His mouth opened. Nothing came out.

Suddenly he pitched forward and Norm cried out, catching him as he fell. Norm was a strong lad, young and fit, but in the end he had to ease him gently to the ground.

You can't hold a dead man for long, Jazz thought.

Towards the end of her nine-hour shift, Jazz sat with Donald in the holding room.

'Donald, your family have reported you missing,' she said. 'I spoke to your wife. She's really worried about you. They all miss you. Your wife. Your daughter. Your grandson. Remember them?'

He looked confused. 'My family?'

She showed him the boarding card in her hand. 'They're all going to be waiting for you in Boston, Donald. The airline that brought you here is going to take you back.' He looked uncertainly at the boarding card. 'We're going to put you on a plane, okay?' Jazz said. 'And your family will be waiting for you at the other end.'

'Okay.'

Jazz stood up to leave.

'But what happened to me?' he said. 'What the hell happened to me?'

Jazz was on the verge of telling him about being refused and removed. Why it happened. What it meant.

But she knew that wasn't really what he was asking about, so she just gave him a little smile, and she said nothing.

Jazz walked Megan to her gate.

With her rucksack and her hair tied back, she suddenly seemed very young. It was the final call for boarding.

'Listen,' Jazz said. 'Listen to me, Megan. It keeps. It does. If it's real, then it doesn't just fade away overnight.'

Megan sighed and handed over her boarding card to the attendant at boarding. When the ticket stub was handed back to her, she stared at it thoughtfully.

'And you know this – how?' she said. 'Because of you and the *We Will Rock You* guy?'

'Just trust me on this one,' Jazz said. 'If he loves you, and if it's meant to be, then he'll wait. Okay?'

Megan looked at her and then looked quickly away, her eyes shining with tears. They were closing the gate.

'You better go now,' Jazz said. 'Maybe I'll see you again one day.'

'Yes,' Megan said. 'Thanks.'

Jazz watched her board the aircraft. There was a flight attendant in the doorway, anxious to shut it in preparation for take-off. Megan turned to wave goodbye.

'What's he called?' Jazz said. 'What's the name of your English boyfriend?'

The American girl had a lovely smile.

'Harry,' she said. 'His name is Prince Harry.'

Five

No Tower for Old Men

Through the smoked glass of the control tower, the Jumbo 747 first revealed itself to Spike as if it were a star above a distant manger, a glittering point of white light in the ink-blue sky.

It was the hour before dawn on a midsummer's day and Spike loved this moment.

Because the star was always getting bigger, and getting closer, and the naked eye of the young man in the Air Traffic Control tower could make out other stars, other bright pinpoints of light stacked up behind it, and he knew that these lights were the first arrivals of the new day, the night flights from Hong Kong, Singapore and Bangkok.

There was a bank of screens before Spike but his eyes were on the sky, and the pinpoints of light above the distant London skyline.

There were three 200-ton planes up there – twenty-five miles away, twenty miles away and fifteen miles away respectively – their nine hundred passengers coming awake to see the sprawl of London beneath them. Three giant aircraft, heading this way at the end of their journey through the night.

And young Spike was going to land them all safe and sound before he had his morning macchiato.

Now he looked at the bank of screens. The Jumbo from Hong Kong appeared as a flight number – BA26 – an altitude – 9000 feet – and the ID of the airport where it was landing – LL for Heathrow. Just a bunch of letters and numbers on a screen, moving with the jerkiness of some video game from the last century. Spike looked at it, and he registered the information, but it was almost subconscious. The most important screen, Spike always said, was the window.

And now a shadow passed across it.

Spike ignored the shadow.

But Earl, Spike's lighting operator, stirred at the sight of the shadow falling across the window. Earl was sitting on the lower level of the tower, the perimeter, and from up on the podium Spike heard his lighting operator chuckle to himself.

'Final approach,' Spike said calmly to the pilot of the 747. It was no longer a shining light in a summer sky but a recognizable wide-body four-engine aircraft capable of flying 345 people across 8000 miles at over 600 miles an hour without once touching the ground. 'Speedbird 26 established on Instrument Landing System,' Spike said. 'Continue approach, clear to land. Wind speed thirty knots at fourteen hundred feet. Stand eighteen. Follow the greens.'

The 747 came out of the sky. Earl had lit up a string

of green lights that would guide the pilot safely to his aircraft's designated stand. These were the greens – a unique lighting system that meant that nobody was going to hit the 747, and he was not going to hit anything.

'Left on Bravo, hold on Link four-one-seven,' Spike said. 'Follow the greens.'

'The shadow's back,' Earl said. 'Check it out, Spike.'

Finally Spike looked at the shadow on the glass.

There was a window cleaner on the outside of the Air Traffic Control tower. Some skinny youth in his early twenties who had been there for most of the week, making their massive smoked-glass window spotless, clipped to a hydraulic lift with massive squeegees attached to his wrist. The cab at the top of the tower was angled out so he was always leaning backwards as he worked with his squeegees nearly ninety metres above the ground.

'That's got to be a stressful job,' Spike said to himself.

They decided to give the window cleaner a cup of tea before they got busy. Spike and Earl had tried waving to him a few times, but he had always looked away, hiding bashfully behind his squeegees. And this was a good time to bring him in.

The first flight of the day, the 747 from Hong Kong, had arrived on time just before five in the morning. Traffic would be light for another hour, and then at six the heavens would open with forty-six planes arriving every hour and another fifty-four departing.

Earl went to get the window cleaner while Spike

watched the sky. He kept watching it when he heard the voice from the other side of the podium.

'Make sure your guest keeps his bucket outside,' the voice said drily.

Spike smiled to himself. 'Don't worry about it, Ian,' he said. 'It's cool.'

'Jolly good,' said the dry voice.

Ian was the oldest controller in the tower. Spike, who was twenty-three, and the youngest, although not by much, had no idea exactly how old Ian might be, but he knew it was like forty or fifty or something. That old. Dad old. Ian liked all the old bands like The Smiths.

They would be sharing duties on the watch. Spike would take care of arrivals on the north runway, while Ian would be taking care of departures on the south runway. So they would be *almost* sharing duties, Spike thought. Nobody liked to admit it, but arrivals were a tougher gig than departures – getting them on the ground needed faster reflexes than getting them in the air. Ian was a good controller, Spike thought. Maybe even a great controller. But he was not twenty-three any more. And if you were an air traffic controller at Heathrow, the world's busiest airport, then you were playing in the Premiership.

Earl appeared with the young window cleaner. The kid had two security clearance cards around his neck – one for cleaning windows airside, and the other for having his cup of tea in the tower. He turned slowly around, taking in the panoramic, 360-degree view of the airfield. Then he looked at them. His mouth fell open.

'I'm Spike. This is Earl.'

The window cleaner stared at them, dumbfounded. Spike and Earl looked at each other and laughed. Because they knew exactly what he was thinking: *Who are these kids?* Spike in his frayed T-shirt and cargo shorts and scuffed Asics, a martial arts tattoo on one arm. And Earl with his shoulder-length hair, sawn-off jeans and bare feet. Oh, they knew what the window cleaner was thinking: *But where are all the grown-ups?*

'Thanks for cleaning our window,' Spike said. 'You're doing an awesome job out there.'

From the outside Spike always thought the control tower looked like an Olympic torch – the long column and then the smoked glass cab on top, tapering out. But when you were going up and down inside, it was like a lighthouse. A long way up. Earl gave the kid a cup of tea. He had earned it.

'I saw that movie,' the window cleaner said. 'That movie about . . . all of this.'

Spike smiled. He knew what he was going to say.

'*Pushing Tin*?' the window cleaner said. 'I saw that movie three times. Did you see it?'

Spike and Earl both nodded, trying not to smirk. They didn't want to hurt the kid's feelings, or to make him think that they were laughing at him. All controllers had seen *Pushing Tin*. It was like people who worked in record shops going to see *High Fidelity*, or gangsters going to see *The Godfather*.

'*Welcome to my sky!*' Spike and Earl quoted in unison, and then they cracked up.

They loved that film in the tower. They thought it

was a fantastic comedy. So wonderfully, gloriously, hilariously wrong. The controllers in that film – they have fights, they have mental breakdowns, they sweat, they drool and they sing. Spike had never seen any air traffic controller do any of those things.

But the biggest travesty in *Pushing Tin*, Spike thought, was that all those controllers were just so *old*.

All those geezers with their weekend barbecues and their marital problems and their bald patches and their meetings with teachers about problem children and their potbellies.

Where did all that come from? Air Traffic Control was a young man's game. But Spike couldn't say any of that. Not with Ian on his watch.

Ian was so old he remembered when the tower was actually landside, half the current size and built of red brick, back in ancient history when dinosaurs walked the earth. About, oh, three years ago.

'That film is not *completely* accurate,' Spike said diplomatically. 'I think you'll find that nobody ever raises their voice up here.'

'But it must be so stressful,' the window cleaner said, shaking his head. 'All those lives in your hands . . .'

Spike smiled.

'If it was stressful,' he said calmly, 'you couldn't do it. Excuse me.'

He looked at the screen and at the sky, and he heard the rollers on Earl's chair glide across the carpet and into position.

'BA12, seven miles from marker, maintain three thousand till intercepting the localizer,' said Spike, and his voice was soothing, hypnotic, designed to inspire trust. 'Descend and maintain five thousand. Reduce speed to one hundred and sixty knots. Clear to land . . . and follow the greens.'

He looked again at the young window cleaner.

'There is no stress,' Spike said. 'But there is urgency. Time is everything. You can't occupy the runway too long at Heathrow.'

He looked over at Ian. He was sitting perfectly still in the twilight of the tower, watching the aircraft at their stands. Here was another reason why arrivals were tougher than departures. Noise restrictions meant planes were allowed to land a lot earlier than they were allowed to leave. Ian hadn't even started work yet.

'Follow the greens,' Spike told the flight from Singapore when it was on the ground. 'Turn left on Echo and park on three-two-two.'

A voice crackled over the intercom.

'But our gate's over here,' objected the pilot.

Spike had been expecting a British or possibly an Australian accent, but the voice was American. Spike exchanged a look with Earl. The lighting operator knew how Spike felt about American pilots. They sometimes confused themselves with kings of the wild frontier. *Follow the greens* was such a simple order, and it ensured that everyone was cocooned from harm, with none of the drama and trauma that happened at lesser airports.

'Follow the greens, turn left on Echo and park on three-two-two,' Spike repeated, firmer this time.

'Or you're going to get lost,' Earl muttered.

The sun was up and dazzling now. The window cleaner shielded his eyes as he watched Spike up on the podium, and it was as if the kid was blinded, not by the rising sun, but by the presence of the young air traffic controller. Spike looked down from the podium and spoke in that voice as soft as a prayer.

'What's your name?' he asked.

The window cleaner's cup seemed to tremble. 'Dan,' he said.

'Dan,' Spike repeated. 'And am I right in thinking that you do not want to clean windows for the rest of your life?'

'Not that there's anything wrong with cleaning windows,' Earl said.

'Absolutely,' Spike agreed. 'But I don't think you want to do it forever. Am I right, Dan?'

The window cleaner's voice was barely audible. 'No,' he said.

'What do you want to do with your life, Dan?'

'I want – I want to keep working here at the airport,' he said, and the words tumbled out as Spike smiled and nodded encouragement. 'The airport makes me feel – I don't know how to say it – like I'm connected to the rest of the world.'

'We understand,' Spike said.

'You do?'

'Of course,' Spike said. 'Look – our game is changing. Controllers used to work their way up from the regional airports. Not any more. Air traffic is increasing, the sky is more crowded. You can go from college door to landing seven hundred aircraft in a working day. Excuse me for a moment, Dan.'

It was an Airbus 380 coming in from Dubai – a double-decker, four-engined, wide-bodied liner, the largest passenger aircraft in the world. And when Spike thought about it later, there was no good reason for what happened.

Weather conditions were perfect. Visibility was good. The runway was dry. But the Airbus landed heavily, and Spike heard the plane's twenty-two wheels shriek with protest, and he saw the nose tyres burst in an explosion of rubber.

'That plane!' said the window cleaner.

'Drink your tea,' Spike told him quietly, as he hit the big red crash button connecting Air Traffic Control to the two fire stations, the police and the Star Centre. 'Airbus 380 on north runway with burst nose-wheel tyres,' he said.

His voice betrayed no emotion, but huge chunks of rubber were strewn across the runway and already Spike could see the orange lights of the vehicles from Airside Ops rushing to the scene.

'I'm holding everything at the stand,' Ian said from the other side of the tower. 'Give me everything you've got, Spike.'

And that was how they did it.

Ian immediately stopped all departures from moving. Spike put his arrivals into a holding pattern and then began diverting them to the clear runway where Ian landed them. Although its front wheels were shot, the Airbus still had twenty more and Earl told the pilot to follow the greens as he guided him to an emergency stand.

Airside Ops had men and equipment on the runway in minutes, including a sweeper to clear shards of rubber that could be fatal if sucked into a jet engine at 1000 centigrade. But there was a huge slab of rubber the size of a man that they could not lift. Then, as Spike watched, one of the Airside Ops team slung it over his shoulder and carried it from the runway.

The fire rigs and the ambulances were standing by, but they were not needed. When Airside Ops had the runway clear of foreign object debris, Ian started moving his departures and Spike was ready for arrivals. The entire drama lasted for five minutes. No flights were delayed.

There was an SAS flight coming in from Stockholm that had been circling the airport. Spike could see it lazily drifting across the sky.

'SK525, you are now clear to land,' Spike said. And then – although he hated to digress from the polite efficiency of Air Traffic Control, he felt that he should add something. 'And thank you for your patience, SK525.'

'No problem,' came a woman's voice. Perfect English but with the faintest accent. 'We're just getting some sightseeing up here,' she said. 'It's a beautiful day, isn't it?'

Spike laughed.

'Yes, it is, SK525,' he said. 'A beautiful day.'

And Spike wondered what she looked like.

He glanced over at Ian and watched him effortlessly

get a perfect line on departures. One aircraft took off, climbed and banked to the right, then one took off, climbed and flew straight ahead, then one took off, climbed and banked to the left. One right, one straight ahead, one left. One right, one straight ahead, one left. It was lovely work. The calm ordering of the planes gave Spike a warm feeling – like when his pen was parallel to the side of his desk, or when all the cans in the cupboard of his flat were as carefully lined up as tin soldiers.

'Clear for take-off, runway twenty-seven left,' Ian said calmly, and Spike realized that he had learned his tone of chilled serenity from this man.

'Ian?'

'What?'

'Thanks,' Spike said.

Ian smiled. 'It's nothing,' he said. The older man peered at him above his reading glasses. 'I've seen burst nose-wheel tyres a hundred times.'

Spike had seen them once.

And suddenly Spike understood that the biggest problem of all with *Pushing Tin* was that they were all in their own little worlds – as individual and alone as boxers. But the best watch in ATC would always have a mix of quick-thinking kids and old men who had seen it all and loved all the old bands like The Smiths.

Spike looked at the window cleaner.

'I wouldn't trade what I do for the world,' Spike said, feeling the need for a summing up. 'But this job is not for everyone. Even good controllers don't always settle at Heathrow. They come from some quiet little backwater, like Luton or Stansted, and they just can't stand the pace. But if you're serious, I can tell you how to go about getting a controller licence.'

Dan smiled shyly. 'Actually, what I really want to be is a pilot.'

Spike stared at him. 'A pilot?' he said.

He heard Ian laugh behind him.

'To be up above the clouds, looking down on the world in all its glory,' Dan said, his eyes getting a dreamy, faraway look. 'To walk through the airport in my uniform and have everyone look at me . . .' He held up his teacup. 'Any chance of a biscuit?'

'No,' Spike said, his voice suddenly coated with the thick ice that he used when some American pilot was reluctant to follow the greens. 'No chance of a biscuit.'

When Earl had taken the window cleaner away, Ian came and stood next to Spike. For a while they said nothing, just watched the lights of the aircraft in the distance, and when Ian spoke he did not take his eyes from the sky.

'He would never have made it anyway,' Ian said. 'He was a bit old.'

Six

The Young Man and the Sky

It was training day and the man and the boy were out on the apron. They both wore tabards – sleeveless high-visibility jackets in orange and yellow. On the back of the man's tabard were the words: TRAINING OFFICER. On the back of the boy's tabard, there was nothing.

'Well?' the man said.

They had their backs to the parked aircraft and they were staring at a neatly clipped patch of grass. There was a bird on the grass. The man and the boy looked at the bird. And the bird looked back.

'Any idea what that might be?' the man said.

The boy looked at the man, a faint smile growing on his lips. It was his first day on the job and he suspected this might be a trick question. A bit of gentle fun at the expense of the new kid. Like when he had worked on a building site one summer and been told to fetch a left-handed hammer.

But the man wasn't smiling.

And so the boy's smile died. He concentrated on the bird. It had a chocolate-brown smudge on its white head. Long red bill and twiglet legs. It was just a bird. It stared back at him with beady black eyes, as if relishing his discomfort.

'Well, it's a bird,' the boy said, thinking it good to make a start.

The man was as unblinking as the bird.

'What kind of bird?' he said with an appalled sigh.

The bird made the harsh noise that passed for its song – a choked, cackling sound that did something to the nerves of the boy's teeth. He was starting to feel agitated.

'Does it matter?' the boy said.

The man watched a 777 take to the skies.

'Oh, you can't imagine how much it matters,' said the man. 'Because we can't get shot of it unless we know what kind of bird it is, see?'

'All right,' said the boy.

'And because bird control is our responsibility,' said the man. 'And because aircraft and birds don't mix. And because we are only as efficient as our least able worker.'

The boy felt his face grow red.

But the man twisted the knife.

'Our least able worker,' he said. 'Guess who that might be?'

The 777 disappeared into clouds and the man looked back at the boy. They could not have been more physically different. The man was lean and wiry with close-cropped hair. The boy towered above him – a big, soft bear of a lad, tall and strong with soft wheat-coloured curls wreathed like laurels around his chubby head. 'Puppy fat,' his mother would murmur lovingly as she brought him second helpings.

Yes, the man and the boy were different in every way. And yet when they had first met, at the interview for the job at Airside Operations, the boy had believed that he and the man were exactly alike.

Because at his interview, the man had spotted the boy for exactly what he was – an aircraft addict. One of those boys who saw planes at an early age and fell in love with them, hard and forever.

'At the age of ten I would bunk off school, bring sandwiches and Coke to the airport to watch the planes,' the boy had told the man. 'And – you know – to be amazed.'

The man had smiled in recognition.

'To be amazed,' he had said. 'Yes. That's it, isn't it?'

'Mates came with me,' the boy said, and he realized that he had never really been able to talk about this before, not with his parents or his girlfriend or anyone until he met the man. 'We would play football with a table tennis ball on top of the multi-storey car park.' His big, soft face fell at the memory of a lonely time. 'Then my mates drifted away,' he said. 'To football, to music, to girls. But I stuck with it. I kept coming to the airport. On their school exercise books, my mates wrote the names of bands and football teams. I had a Pan Am baggage sticker.'

The man had let the boy ramble on because of course he had done it too, twenty years earlier – pedalled his bike out to Heathrow, pressed his face against the wire and watched the giant, dolphin-smooth planes roar overhead for hours and hours; and yet somehow it was never enough. The man understood. This place was not an airport. It was a cathedral – built to inspire awe. The boy had gazed upon the cathedral, and been suitably awed.

'An anorak,' the boy had said, and for the first time a cloud passed across the man's lean face.

'I don't like that term,' he had said. 'Anorak. It's derogatory.'

'Trainspotter?' the boy had offered, trying to win back the feeling of easy fraternity. 'Planespotter?'

'Too flippant,' the man had said. 'I like . . . enthusiast.'

They shook hands and the boy – that big lad, that gentle giant, that lifelong enthusiast – had the job of his dreams in Airside Ops.

The boy had inevitably thought the interview signalled the start of a beautiful friendship. Days and nights discussing Concorde, the World War Two origins of the Double Sunrise Club, and year zero – the birth of Heathrow itself, with the opening of London Airport on 1st January 1946.

But no.

Loving Concorde, knowing about the Double Sunrise Club, getting a warm feeling at the thought of the airport rising in the aftermath of the war – suddenly it wasn't enough. The rides to the airport on his bike – all at once they counted for nothing. His first day at work and he had to prove himself. With this bloody bird.

'Is it . . . a seagull?'

The man told the boy to follow him back to their vehicle. When they were settled inside, the boy watched the bird through the windscreen, searching for clues.

The man tapped the dashboard.

'Look at that,' he said.

There was a dial on the dashboard and at every point on the dial there was the name of a kind of bird. It seemed to the boy that every bird in existence was there. Crow. Rook. Starling. Lapwing. Magpie. Pigeon. Gulls had an entire section to themselves. Black-headed gull. Common gull. Herring gull.

'You see "seagull" anywhere on there?' the man said.

The boy's gentle blue eyes flitted around the dial once, and then again. There was no point on the dial where a seagull was mentioned.

'No,' he said.

'That's because seagulls don't exist,' the man said, sucking in his upper lip. 'Lesson one – *there is no such thing as a seagull.*'

He turned the dial to the point where it said 'black-headed gull' and adjusted some buttons that said BIRDS – FUNCTION – SOUND LEVEL.

From the speakers on top of the vehicle came a dreadful sound – the harsh, cackling noise that the bird had made, and yet somehow worse.

The bird stiffened with alarm. It took to the air, fluttered briefly towards the Airside Ops vehicle and then flew away.

'That's the sound of a black-headed gull in distress,' the man said. 'We get all sorts here. Kestrels. Starlings. Canadian geese. Swans. Common gulls. Black-headed

78

gulls. Herring gulls. But no seagulls yet.' He paused for thought. 'Although I think I might have seen a dodo once,' he said.

The boy ignored the cheap shot.

'Do they really sound so different?' he asked.

The man made a rat-like squeaking noise. 'Pigeon,' he said. Then he made a sound like a duck being strangled. 'Rook,' he said. 'They sound alike to you?'

'Not really,' the boy confessed.

They watched another bird idling on the grass.

'They love the grass,' the man said.

'Then why don't we get rid of the grass?' the boy said.

'Surface water,' the man said. 'The grass does its job soaking up the English rain. But we keep it cut from eight to twelve inches – they don't like that length.' He shook his head and laughed at the bird strutting and preening in the grass. 'Look at him. Loafing about. The airport is a big open space, great for all the stuff birds like to do – eating, drinking, sleeping, breeding, and loafing around. What about you? Do you like loafing around?'

'What? Me? No!'

'Good,' the man said. 'So – we get rid of the birds. We have our sound system of birds in distress. We have air rifles, pistols and shotguns. We have our horn.' He leaned on the car's horn, to demonstrate. 'And some-times we just get out of the vehicle and flap our arms.'

The boy couldn't tell if this was a joke or not.

'We do what it takes to keep the airport safe,' the man said, glancing at his watch. 'The birds are just a part of it.'

'I never knew that birds were so different,' the boy said, making an effort to please the man.

The man nodded.

'The crow is an intelligent bird,' he said. 'Kestrels – the kestrel is a singular bird. I have a grudging admiration for the kestrel. But some birds are just thick,' the man said, and he looked meaningfully at the boy out of the corner of his eye.

Later they were parked directly in front of an Airbus 380, more like an ocean liner than a plane, its giant wings with the four mighty engines bowed with the weight of 215,000 litres of aviation fuel.

'A plane has its own body language,' the man said, so quietly that they could have been sitting in a church. 'There are no indicators on a plane. A plane cannot tell you that it is about to turn left into Acacia Avenue. But a plane talks. A plane says volumes. You just need to know how to listen. The red light on a plane is on the port side – the side the captain sits. The white lights are the tail lights. So any pilot in any country in the world can immediately determine which way a plane is flying from those red and white lights. Aircraft are not cars, buses or trains. They are four hundred tons of fun flying at forty thousand feet with five hundred human beings inside. And there are lots of them.'

They considered the gargantuan Airbus 380.

'The flaps are angled down on this here Airbus,' the man said. 'Know why?'

'For take-off,' the boy said.

'Know how you tell an Airbus from a Boeing?'

'An Airbus has wing tips,' the boy said. 'Boeings do not. And an Airbus has a chisel tail and a tick-shaped cockpit window.'

The boy waited for a compliment, no matter how mild or reluctant. But the man was squinting at the sky.

'Swallows and swifts,' he said. 'Summer birds. Aerial feeders and breeders. Got to keep your eye on those loafers.'

'All right,' said the boy. 'I will.'

The man filled his lungs with air and sighed. The boy could smell it too. Above the smell of the freshly cut grass that was always there, and the smell of the burning rubber that the aircraft tyres left on the runway when they came in for landing, there was the special airport smell – like an ocean made of kerosene.

'Jet A-1,' the man said. 'Aviation fuel. I love it.' He sighed again. 'The smell of Jet A-1 at the end of a summer's day.'

The boy loved it too.

And above their heads, the crowded sky roared.

The boy found what he was looking for in an airside bookshop.

On a shelf devoted to the attractions of Britain, surrounded by guides to London, the Lake District and the Highlands, next to a long shelf where Kate and William smiled their dazzling smiles, there was a brightly coloured paperback called *The RSPB Birds of Britain and Europe*. And the boy thought – RSPB? Royal Society for the Prevention of Birds?

81

He had never known they were so hated.

The cover alone had enough birds to study for a lifetime. There were birds of every size, shape and colour. Birds that the boy had never heard of and a few that he had. Puffin. Grey heron. Turtle dove. Herring gull. Kestrel. They were arranged in neat lines, all pictured in profile, like a series of mugshots, or feathered suspects in a police identification parade. Criminality – that was the general impression.

A pilot came in and asked one of the shop assistants if they had a poetry section. But they didn't have a poetry section. The pilot left looking disappointed, absent-mindedly adjusting the peak of his cap.

The boy bought the bird book and began to study it during his lunch break when he was in the Airside Ops cabin, eating the stack of sandwiches that his mother had made for him to keep his strength up. When he lifted his eyes from the police line-up of birds, the man was watching him with his large, unblinking eyes.

'Any good?' the man asked quietly.

The boy showed him the cover. 'It's specifically written for those starting out on their birdwatching journey,' he said.

The man nodded.

'You know why I'm so hard on you?' he asked the boy.

But the boy had no idea.

'Because you don't have your nose pressed up against the fence any more,' said the man. 'Now you're in Airside Ops. We're responsible for the safety and efficiency of arrivals and departures. Heathrow carries seventy million passengers a year. But Airside Ops carries none. Get it? Not one passenger is carried by Airside Operations. We can't afford to carry passengers.'

They looked at each other for a long moment.

'This book,' the boy said. 'It's a good book. It's by the Royal Society for the Prevention of Birds.'

The man stared at him for a while.

'Great tit,' the man said.

The boy felt his face turn red.

The man impatiently tapped the cover of the boy's book. He was pointing at a small yellow bird on the top line of the cover, parked between a jay and a chaffinch.

'Great tit,' the man repeated. 'The bird. Who did you think I was talking about?'

They went everywhere.

The great divide airside was between the apron and manoeuvring. Double white lines marked the gap between the apron, where aircraft were parked, serviced and maintained, and manoeuvring, where the action was – the taxiways, the grass areas and the airport's two runways.

Men roamed the apron alone. But out where the aircraft came and went, they always manoeuvred in pairs: two vehicles containing two-man teams. Four times a day they inspected the runways for FOD – foreign object debris – which could be anything, anything at all, from a paper clip to an engine. Seen from up close, the runways were spotless. Seen from up close, the boy could have eaten his stack of sand-wiches off the runways. Airside Ops kept them that way. When he learned the call signals of the two vehicles looking for FOD on the runways, the boy stared at the man in surprise.

'Checker and . . . Seagull?' he said.

'That's it,' the man said, turning onto the north runway. In the distance they could see the other vehicle. 'That's Checker and we're Seagull.'

'But I thought that seagulls don't exist,' the boy said.

'They don't,' the man said. 'Probably someone's idea of a little joke.'

A giant Airbus 380 was coming in and they got out of the way, parking by a red-and-white blast barrier to watch it pass. The man squinted at the Airbus with eyes that had watched a million landings. And he shook his head. The boy knew that something wasn't right.

'That's going to hurt in the morning,' the man said, and they saw the undercarriage come down hard directly in front of them, and watched the nose wheels touch the runway and the tyres immediately explode into a shower of flying red-hot rubber. Before the boy had breathed out, the man was already talking to the duty manager on the bridge at the Airside Ops control room.

'Crash box, Rod,' he said.

Then they were out on the runway. Ahead of them, the Airbus was following the greens on its remaining twenty tyres and they could hear Air Traffic Control diverting all landings to the other runway, and holding departures at their stands. All hands at Airside Ops were out on the runway, sweeping up the burning rubber that was scattered everywhere. They could see the lights of the fire service hurtling towards them. And, exactly where the Airbus had landed, the two lads from Checker were struggling to lift a slab of smoking rubber the size and weight of a very large man.

'We're going to need special gear to shift that thing,' the man told his duty manager. 'And tell them to shut the runway.'

But they didn't need special gear.

The boy told the lads from Checker to stand back. Then he crouched down and wrapped his arms around the slab of steaming rubber as if it was a living thing that he needed to subdue.

Straining with every sinew of his substantial being, his eyes squeezed shut and the veins in his neck and forehead pulsing, the boy struggled up, the rubber locked in his arms, his legs almost buckling, the steam rising off him. Crying out with the effort, he threw the hunk of burning rubber onto his back and began to half-walk, half-stagger to a grass area. There he collapsed onto the grass, flat on his back, the giant slice of aircraft tyre still smouldering by his side.

The man laughed with delight.

'Runway's open, Rod,' he said into his radio. 'All clear down here.'

The man went over to the boy. High above the airport, the man could already see aircraft coming out of their holding patterns. He saw the blue glint of an SAS tail fin caught by the sun as it descended for landing. He looked across at the lads from Checker. They both smiled and shook their heads.

'You did good,' the man told the boy.

The boy got up onto his elbows. He was still fighting for breath, but the man could see he wanted to say something. The man leaned closer.

'See that?' the boy said.

The man followed his gaze. Twenty yards away, a fierce-looking bird with brown plumage was watching them. Its vicious-looking beak was clearly designed for tearing living flesh, but its large black eyes gave it a perplexed, almost gentle appearance.

'What about it?' said the man.

'That's a kestrel,' said the boy,

At night the airport glittered like a box of jewels poured out by some careless god.

There was the hard-red glow and diamond-white lights of the planes that came out of the darkness until close to midnight. There was the golden haze of the landing lights. The steady orange throb of the warning lights on the airside vehicles. The bright green lights that guided the aircraft from the runway to their stand. And Terminal 5 all lit up like a tree on Christmas Eve.

And when it came to the moment when there would be no more aircraft until the giants arrived from Asia with the dawn, the boy thought that the airport seemed like a ghost town from the future, or an abandoned civilization from another planet. It was beautiful. And as he drove the vehicle around the apron, he knew that the man saw it too.

The boy stopped to look at the tail of a 777 sticking out of a hangar.

'The planes are getting bigger,' the man said. 'But the hangars are still the same size.'

And they laughed in perfect harmony.

When the snows came, they were ready.

Airside Ops worked all through the night to clear the runways and taxiways of the airport. Eighteen months into the job, it had been the boy's first red snow alert, the highest level of snow warning at Heathrow, and when dawn crept in, grey and misty and freezing, he leaned against the big yellow tractor he had been driving all night, so weak with exhaustion that he thought he must be seeing things.

But the man saw it too. And so did the new kid.

It was standing in one of the grass areas near the runway. It was like some small statue that had been created by the night, as erect and unmoving as a tin soldier, as white as the drifts of snow they had pushed from the runways and taxiways. The boy thought of a book he remembered from his childhood, where the good creatures of the forest were all turned to stone by the wicked witch of winter.

'I've never seen that before,' the man said. 'In all my years, I have never seen that before.'

'A bird,' the boy said. 'Frozen solid.'

'Wow,' said the new kid. 'That poor seagull.'

The man and the boy had a good chuckle at that.

They told the new kid to go to one of the Airside Ops vehicles and have a look at the dial on the dashboard and see if he could find the distress call for a seagull. But as the new kid trudged wearily back to the car, something passed between the man and the boy.

They both knew that the new kid would be all right.

He had worked hard and well and uncomplaining all through the black, freezing night. But more than this, the new kid had ridden his bike to the wire as a child. He had bunked off school to come to the airport, for the same reason that the man and the boy and all of them had come to the airport in their long-lost childhoods.

To be amazed.

Seven

Final Call

Damon pulled back the curtains of their hotel room and the airport was there.

Even at first light, the place was teeming with life. He could see the red, white and blue tail fin of a big British Airways 777 wheeling off the runway towards its stand and, if he craned his neck, there were the lights of the aircraft coming out of the sky, stacked up neatly for landing. A purple pod scuttled by his window and he rubbed his eyes, unsure if he had imagined it. Then another one scuttled by – these little purple pods that looked like some ancient sci-fi vision of the future.

The sight of all this activity made his spirits dip. He had hoped to be up before the rest of the world. But the day, this special day, had already begun.

His wife, Liz, stirred at the light in the window. He heard her rise from their bed and go through the adjoining door to their daughters, Saskia, eleven, and Edie, just turned nine. He heard small, tired voices, and the dog bark twice.

'Is it time?' he heard the oldest girl say.

'Yes,' his wife said gently. 'It's time to go home.'

89

They were an Australian family who had lived in London for ten years. Edie had been born here, and Saskia had been one year old when they arrived. To both of them, Australia meant grandparents, cousins and sunshine on Christmas Day. They loved it well enough, but it was a place they went to on holiday. They were Londoners.

Schools, friends, memories and the ten thousand ties that bind – they were all here. Damon had become a Londoner too. And so had Liz. And he thought that while you could never become English, and while it was not easy to even become British in a mere ten years, you could certainly become a Londoner. For him the process had begun here – at London's airport.

Damon had travelled the world for business and knew that airports were often just the punctuation marks of a lifetime, the twilight spaces between places and people, the no-man's-land between what had happened and what was yet to be. But they could be much more than that. The airport could be where a new life began. He had learned that at Heathrow.

Damon remembered the immigration officer who had taken their passports when they arrived. Out of their minds from twenty-four hours of flying, their one-year-old screaming the roof down, his wife sick and heavily pregnant. The immigration officer – a small blonde woman, very young – had taken their daughter's stuffed toy – a particularly charmless monkey called Curious George – and used it to stamp their Australian passports. The child had stopped crying immediately and had been rendered speechless by this magical place where a monkey might stamp you in at passport control. And Damon had never forgotten that small, kind gesture; it had set the tone for ten years of happiness.

His youngest daughter appeared by his side, blinking away the sleep. Edie was fair-haired, very slim, which they all put down to her fussy eating. Damon put his arm around her and she was still warm inside her pyjamas. The thought that this place was where her life had begun moved him deeply.

'Look at this,' he said, gesturing at the airport. 'I want you to remember this forever.'

They stared at the airport together.

'But I don't see anything,' said the child, in her London accent.

The immigration officer who had stamped their Australian passports with Curious George was at that very moment chasing a large lady from Lagos into a toilet.

Jazz and Norm had been waiting for the woman at the gate of her flight from Amsterdam, but she had bolted at the sight of their UKBA flashes. Jazz had managed to grab the woman's coat – long and black, despite the summer heat – but she had shrugged her off.

Now drawing herself up to her full five foot two inches, Jazz contemplated the large lady from Lagos as the woman turned to face her, finding herself cornered inside the toilet.

The lining of the woman's coat was ripped where Jazz had tried to hold her. Thick wads of five hundred and one thousand Nigerian Naira bank notes, shiny and purple, were spilling out of the torn coat and fluttering across the floor. There was also something white and bony and dead inside the lining – an animal's head, a voodoo talisman, a fetish for warding off evil spirits, and its empty eye sockets seemed to stare right through Jazz.

The large lady from Lagos removed a document from her pocket – an e-ticket, it looked like – and took a tentative nibble at the corner.

'To be honest with you,' Jazz told her, 'I don't even know where to start.'

Jazz heard a nervous cough behind her and realized that Norm had stayed outside.

'You're allowed inside the ladies' toilet on special occasions, Norm,' Jazz called without turning round. 'You have police powers, remember.'

She heard his shy footsteps approaching but did not take her eyes from the large lady from Lagos. The woman took a bigger bite of her e-ticket.

'Stop that now,' Jazz said, giving her the flinty look that preceded physical contact. 'Don't make me take you down.'

The large lady from Lagos chuckled to herself and took a massive bite of her e-ticket.

Jazz looked at Norm and shook her head.

'Why do they always laugh when I say that?' Jazz said.

She took three quick paces forward, threw one leg round the back of the woman's calves and shoved her chest with the palms of her hand. The large lady from Lagos came crashing down, and Jazz felt the voodoo talisman crack hard against her shins. It was the skull of a monkey. She recognized it now.

But Jazz would not have recognized the Australian family. The youngest girl hadn't been born when she had greeted them at the border all those years ago. The quiet, poised eleven-year-old had been a squawking baby. The wife, Liz, had still been in her twenties, not much more than a girl herself, and now she was closer to forty than thirty. And the man – he was older too. Yet maybe Jazz would have recognized him, despite ten long years in the City, and she would certainly have understood his sadness at leaving this new home for another, much older home.

But that was the airport, Jazz would have told you. A series of hellos and goodbyes.

And now it was time for goodbye again.

A taxi took them to the Animal Reception Centre.

Damon sat next to the driver while his wife and daughters occupied the backseat, the dog fretting in his big blue container across their laps. The girls tried to comfort the dog and the woman tried to comfort the man. Saskia and Edie cooed the dog's name – Hawkeye – and Liz leaned forward and patted Damon's shoulder twice.

There was a world in that gesture.

It said – But you do know this is the right time to go back, don't you? It said – Look, our parents are still alive, but they are all getting older. It said – You know as well as I do that the boom years are over in this country. It said – Taking the girls back just before the start of their secondary education is the right move, the smart move.

And he knew it was all true.

Yet still he was sad.

And the thought of his father – the loud, shouty arguments at a thousand dinner tables, the piercing look of disappointment that sometimes the old man made no attempt to hide – depressed and oppressed him. But he was grateful for her gesture, and Damon smiled at his wife as they pulled into the nondescript premises of the Heathrow Animal Reception Centre.

The only people in the front office were a diffident young man and a woman who was so beautiful that they all had to look at her three or four times to make sure that they had not imagined her.

Tim checked Hawkeye's paperwork and, satisfied with all of that, he let the dog out of his container and expertly ran his fingers through the fur of his neck. Hawkeye closed his eyes and his mouth fell open with rapture. The thick pink tongue lolled. The beautiful young woman watched Tim comfort the dog, and she seemed to swoon a little bit too.

'We'll take good care of him,' said Tim.

'See you in Sydney, Hawkeye,' said Saskia. 'Only ten thousand five hundred and sixty-five miles to go.'

'Yes, see you in Sydney, Hawkeye,' said Edie. 'See you – tomorrow? The day after tomorrow?'

The girls both looked at their father for the answer.

But Damon was thinking that they already sounded more Australian.

* * *

Karin was a Senior First Officer for SAS, three stripes on the sleeve of her neat blue pilot's jacket. Her immaculate uniform made Spike feel shabby and immature in his T-shirt and cargo shorts. He thought perhaps he should have worn his clean pair of cargo shorts.

She flew to Arlanda, Stockholm, out of Terminal 3 so that is where Spike met her, upstairs at the Café Costa, just down from Departures. She watched him empty three sugars into his espresso, and then line up the empty packets.

'Why do you do that?' she laughed. 'Make everything in the straight lines?'

Her English was perfect and yet somehow – imperceptibly, magically – it was clearly her second language. Even when there was nothing actually wrong with her English, it had an adorable charm that made Spike's heart ache with longing. *Make everything in the straight lines*. There was nothing wrong with that sentence, Spike thought. But it was gloriously, unmistakably her – Captain Karin of SK525, who said she was happy to do a little sightseeing when you asked her to circle the airport.

'I don't know why I do it,' Spike said helplessly. That's how she made him feel – helpless. He was aware it wasn't exactly what women wanted in a man, but he couldn't help himself. 'When are you coming back?' he said.

That wasn't what he wanted to ask her. What he wanted to ask her was – Do you have a boyfriend? Or even a husband? Or an ex-husband? But he did not dare. He liked her far too much to risk hearing the answer.

'I don't know when I'm coming back,' she said, and pulled on her pilot's cap as she stood up. Spike stood up with her. He was a tall young man, over six feet, but their eyes were level. 'You never know your luck,' she said, and laughed happily, as though it was an expression that she had heard in a classroom and always wanted to try out.

'That's right,' Spike said. 'You never know your luck.'

He walked her down to the Departures area. It was a place for goodbyes. A couple kissed as though the world was ending. A boy watched a girl until she was lost beyond the security barrier. A woman wept as a man walked away.

But although he would love her for the rest of his days, this was the first time Spike had met Captain Karin and he was painfully aware that buying her a cappuccino and a chocolate twist did not even give him the right to kiss her cheek.

She held out her hand and he shook it.

'Is not goodbye,' she said, and Spike thought that it was such a wonderful thing to say. He watched her pass through the gate reserved for flight crews. If she looks back, Spike thought, then we will have a child together. If she just looks back . . .

Later, when he was up in the tower, Spike stared down at the stands and watched them ready a Qantas Airbus 380 for its flight to the other side of the planet, and he thought about that film, that terrible film that all the controllers always laughed about. But Spike wasn't laughing now.

Spike thought of the weekend barbecues and the kids on the lawn and the meetings with teachers. He thought about growing older with someone. He thought about a house where you lived with the woman you had chosen, out of all the women in the world, and who had chosen you, out of all the men in the world.

And for the first time in his life, Spike could sort of see the point of it.

There was a clear summer sky above the green plane.

The firefighters hunched below the burning wing, laying down their carpet of foam while flames curled around the giant 747 engine like a fist, sending up thick plumes of black smoke into the bright cloudless blue.

Fire Officer Mike Truman was at the wheel of the rig that faced the nose of the plane and he looked up at the perfect sky and sighed. This weather really ticks me off, he thought. Mike did not know, and could not imagine, what conditions would be like on the day all of this was for real.

Yet he knew it would be nothing like today.

But that was all right. If you don't like the weather, Mike thought, just wait a while. And if you *do* like the weather – well.

Just wait a while.

Damon's black cloud lifted briefly as they were passing through security.

While other more slow-witted travellers set the bells ringing with the buckles on their belts and the small change hidden in their jeans and the metal that dangled forgotten from their necks, wrists and navels, Damon and his family passed deftly through the screenings. Even the children were old hands at this game – removing their shoes without being asked, stuffing their watches into their rucksacks as a matter of course, urging their mother to make sure she had all her liquids and gels in a small, sealable plastic bag.

But when they were airside, it hit him hard. He had passed once again to the other side. Only this time it was different. For this was neither business nor pleasure. A life had started in this airport. And now it was ending.

The night they had left their home, the neighbours had thrown a street party for them. That made it sound far grander and far more planned than it really was; the people next door had knocked with a bottle of champagne, and they had drunk it sitting on the steps, it was such a lovely evening, and soon other neighbours were coming out of their homes and the children were running up and down the quiet North London street and it didn't get dark until ten o'clock and he thought, Oh, we are so mad to leave all this for a country we do not know any more. The airport had that power, he saw. It could measure exactly how much you were losing.

Now Damon stood among the bright, excited bustle of airside, his throat strained with sadness, and watched his daughters putting on their trainers as his wife watched him.

'Hey,' Liz said. 'You.'

Damon looked at her.

'Do you know how much we love you?' she said.

He stared at her for a moment and then he gathered them up in his arms, the three of them, his wife and two daughters, the youngest girl still struggling to get a trainer on, the oldest one asking a question about what he thought the dog was doing right now, and as he held them he knew that home would always be wherever this woman and these two children were, and if you saw them on your way to your flight, if you looked at the little family twice, then you would have thought that it was just one of those scenes that you see a million times every week at the airport.

The sight of someone who is truly beloved, someone who is more loved than they will ever know, coming home at last.

Acknowledgements

At Mischief PR, thank you to Dan Glover and Charlotte Hutley.

At Heathrow, thank you to Cat Jordan and the communications team, Simon Newbold, C Watch, UK Border Agency, Plane Food, British Airways, Heathrow Animal Reception Centre, Heathrow Fire and Police Services and NATS (National Air Traffic Services).

And thanks to all the staff at the Sofitel London Heathrow.

CATCHING THE SUN

When taxi driver Tom Finn is almost jailed for
confronting two burglars in his own home, he leaves
broken Britain and takes his wife and children to live
on the tropical island of Phuket, Thailand.

Phuket is all the Finn family dreamed of –
a tropical paradise where the children swim with
elephants, the gibbons sing love songs in the jungle,
the Andaman Sea is like turquoise glass and this
young family is free to grow.

But both man-made disaster and the unleashed
forces of nature shatter this tropical idyll.

Catching the Sun is a gripping, moving story of
a family who go in search of Paradise – and end
up discovering themselves.

Out in 2012